TALES OF VICTORIAN NORFOLK

MARY MANN

This remarkable collection of short stories about a Norfolk village in the 1890's was written by Mary E. Mann, the wife of Fairman Mann, a substantial Shropham farmer. Well known at the time as a novelist, Mrs. Mann conveyed in these stories, in an unaffected and powerful style, her first-hand experience of Norfolk village life; a life of unremitting toil where the threat of poverty and the workhouse was ever present.

Fashioned with great narrative skill and a subtle humour the object of these tales is truth, truth about poverty, about acts kind and brutal, about childhood, old age and superstition in a Norfolk village of the 19th century.

The stories were selected by the late Ted Goodwyn and John Baxter. Ted Goodwyn also provided an introduction about the life and works of Mary Mann.

*

Stories from this collection were read on BBC Radio 4 in October 2000.

TALES OF
VICTORIAN
NORFOLK

MARY E. MANN

Selected and Introduced by
E. A. Goodwyn & J. C. Baxter

Illustrations by
Mary Nina Walker

Morrow & Co, Bungay, Suffolk
2000

First published Morrow & Co, Bungay, 1991
Reprinted (paperback) 1992
Reprinted (paperback) 2000

ISBN 0 948903 14 7

Printed and bound by Antony Rowe Limited
Chippenham, Wiltshire

CONTENTS

CONTENTS

INTRODUCTION

Reviewing Mary Mann's novel, "The Parish Nurse", in 1905, Hugh Massingham wrote: "Norfolk has in her a writer of whom it may well be proud, who should in time come into her kingdom". The expectation has not been realised; Norfolk's long indifference to Mary Mann is a disgrace. Even when in 1976 the Boydell Press re-printed her best collection of stories, "The Fields of Dulditch" — enthusiastically supported in "The Eastern Daily Press" by Adrian Bell — little notice was taken in the county of her birth, where she spent all her life and of whose people she wrote with such remarkable insight. We venture to hope that this selection of her Norfolk tales, half from "The Fields of Dulditch" and half from her other collections of short stories, may help to realise the expectation raised by Massingham so long ago.

Mary Elizabeth Rackham was born in Norwich in 1848, only daughter of William Simon Rackham, a prosperous Manchester warehouseman. In 1871 she married Fairman Mann of Shropham in south-west Norfolk. He was both landowner and tenant, farming eventually about 800 acres. The Manns lived first at Church Farm and then at Shropham Manor where at least two previous generations of the family had resided. Three daughters and one son were born during the first ten years of the marriage and they were still children when the farmer's wife completed her first novel, "The Parish of Hilby" in 1883. In a letter to her nephew, Tom Fairman Ordish, she describes how she was writing with two little girls on the arms of her chair.

It was Ordish who recognised her talent, encouraged her to write and helped in the publication of her early novels. "It is as certain as anything," she wrote to him, "that I should never have attempted to do more than pester my friends with long letters if it had not been for you."[1] A civil servant based in London, Ordish was both a keen antiquarian and a notable Shakespearean scholar, author of "Early London Theatres" and "Shakespeare's London". He was only six years younger than his aunt; the fact that he kept all the many letters she wrote to him over a period of more than twenty years indicates the strength of his devotion; and he provided for her the only direct contact she had with metropolitan culture. The Manns — there were several Mann families farming in west Norfolk — were worthy folk but indifferent to literature. Now and then some asperity concerning their philistian outlook creeps into the letters to Ordish. And Shropham was a very dull place for a lively and sociable woman.

In the Draft of a Foreword to "The Fields of Dulditch", Mary Mann describes that fictional village, which in fact is Shropham, as "A depressing neighbourhood certainly. As I detail its several features I am appalled at the bleakness, the dreariness of the prospect. And it is certain that we who pass our lives here in the silence and the solitude are not always content. We know that Fate has been to us in much unkind. We know that the Book of Life has been for us, practically, closed; that only tantalisingly and at moments have we been permitted to turn its pages... The deprivation", she concludes, "makes us restless still, bitter at times and reproachful of Fate."

The situation was made far worse for her and the whole

[1] For permission to quote from the letters to Ordish and from the unpublished Foreword to "The Fields of Dulditch", we are indebted to Mrs Diana Hyde, daughter of Surgeon-Commander Fairman Rackham Mann, and granddaughter of Mary Mann.

family by the long depression from which agriculture suffered during the greater part of her literary career. In the draft Foreword she wrote — a passage omitted in the printed version — of the effect upon her husband: "a man well-to-do, kind and generous once; an excellent husband, father, master, farmer: getting now poorer in pocket, shorter in temper, year by year, a man who has struggled in a dogged, quiet fashion, but who is beaten and knows it, finding the knowledge bitter to a degree and self-deteriorative". The plight of men like Fairman Mann was put to the Royal Commission on the Agricultural Depression (1894) by the experienced Norfolk farmer and M.P., C. S. Read: "The condition of farmers in Norfolk is verging on ruin and wholesale bankruptcy.... We have had a good many yeomen in Norfolk and I say they are the hardest hit of all. They have got to bear the losses of the landowner and the losses of the tenant... they have gone to the wall worse by far than the common tenant farmers".[1]

The financial stringency which the depression caused and which bore so heavily upon those accustomed to relative affluence, influenced Mary Mann's writing. Some of her novels are clearly written with the intention to please the popular taste for romance and a happy ending. Making money became an important object in order to sustain an acceptable way of life for the family at the Manor, upon whom, as the Hall was often unoccupied or let for the shooting, the customary responsibilities of a squire's family devolved. Fairman Mann was for many years a Churchwarden, a Guardian, Overseer and both Secretary and Treasurer of the village school — his was always the largest annual subscription — where Mary Mann sometimes helped. She

[1] In a letter to Tom Ordish of June 1885, Ordish having asked for a loan of £20, Fairman Mann wrote enclosing a cheque, but stipulating "When I tell you that I have lost more than £800 this year you will quite understand my shortness of cash and three months hence this £20 I shall want to help to pay my harvest wages".

also provided the fare for the annual school treat held in the great barn at the Manor. Husband and wife took their full share in village life. And it seems certain that during her early years in Shropham, as an attractive young wife with small children, Mary Mann frequently visited the homes of the labourers. How else could she have gained that intimate knowledge of cottage interiors and of the labourers' wives and children which so many of her stories show?

This experience affected her deeply. She found a compensation for the narrowness of her life — and, of course, a fruitful subject for her writing — in opening her heart and mind to the trials and tribulations of the simple poor. Addressing, in the unpublished Foreword, the affluent "who weary of travel or the London season", she asks: "What do you say to the thrilling intelligence that old Roadman Clark has come upon the parish at last? (Bob Clark who has had such a pride in the fact that he has lived for seventy-five years and has never cost the 'Parush' a penny; who asserted so emphatically up to the last that he, be his necessities what they might, he at least would never stoop to become a 'porpoise'): that Martha Allen, the 'pallatic', has had another fit: that a couple of Robinson's short-horns have had to be killed on the Brightlands' Farm: and that anthrax is feared? What do you make of stirring incidents such as these?

Yet do these things move us strongly. Our emotions are stirred as freely by the sorrows of the toilers by field and hedgerow as they might be stirred by the far more sensational tragedies of the street. Perhaps more freely: I cannot say. We may not see and hear and pass on; circumstances compel us to live side by side with the suffering we see, to take the misfortune into our own lives, to feel the oppression in our hearts."

The sympathy she felt did not in the least blind her to the realities of village life. There is no idealisation of it in her stories, and none of that escapism found in much contemporary literature of rural England, as in Eleanor Hayden's "Travels round our Village" (1901): "It is good in these days of bustle and strife, to drift for a while into some quiet backwater — such as may yet be found in rural England — which the tide of progress stirs but just enough to avert stagnation and where old-world customs and archaic forms of speech still linger and where men go about their daily tasks in a spirit of serene leisureliness, therein copying Nature which never hurries. Of such a sequestered corner, its humours, its homely comedies and simple pathos would I write..." Such an attitude was alien to Mary Mann. She certainly bowed to popular taste in various novels, but in her rural tales her object was truth. In this she resembles George Crabbe, the father of East Anglian literature —

> "I paint the cot
> As Truth will paint it, and as bards will not."

Of the evil aspects of village life as she portrays it, two stand out: brutality and superstition. "Ben Pitcher's Elly" exemplifies the first. When Pitcher realises that his daughter "has been a bad hussy", he begins "to busy himself with the belt that was round his waist", but Elly faints before he can start to beat her. When she recovers, he is about to return to work after his dinner — "Don't le' me find you hare, in home o' mine, when I come back ter-night — du I'll kill yer...". Another story of brutality within a family is "The Lost Housen" where, in an isolated cottage, the cruelty of a father to wife and two sons is repaid with savage interest when the father's strength fails; and the story ends with a horrible suicide.

Superstition is prominent in two stories. At the end of "A Dulditch Angel", the poor old man, living alone in his isolated cottage, is persuaded, with tragic consequences, that his recently dead wife has returned in the form of a bat. The malignant power of superstition spread by village gossip is the theme of "The Witch of Dulditch", where a good, kind woman is hounded to suicide.

The aspect of village life which dominates the tales is poverty. It is illustrated most starkly in "Wolf Charlie"and "The Gal La'rences". At the beginning of the former tale, the "three-quarter man" is a lodger. There comes a very hard winter. "The mother was doling out to her half-dozen little children the morning meal of bread soaked in hot water, peppered and salted; of this for the first time she ceased to offer the lodger a share. The poor fellow said no word of remonstrance, of appeal, of farewell even, but turned his back upon the place where his home had been, and on the familiar faces, and took his way along a certain road..." Near-starvation faces him again when he emerges from the workhouse with a "wife" and her five children. Such prolonged abject poverty, with no hope of escape, might seem to make a tale of unrelieved gloom, but it is not altogether so. The dogged endurance of the man compels admiration; and that Mary Mann was acutely aware of the qualities fostered in the Norfolk peasant through generations of deprivation and desperate struggle the tale of "The Gal La'rences" movingly illustrates. The two young women stoically endure extreme hardship not for themselves but for their children. In "A Dulditch Rose" an elderly woman does the same for her fatherless grandson.

Some aspects of village life Mary Mann almost ignored in these stories. Whereas her novels are full of parsons good, not so good and indifferent, in the rural tales religion is of little importance. An ineffectual parson is a minor character in three of them, but her "Studies of the Norfolk Peasant" (the sub-title of "The Fields of Dulditch") suggest general indifference to religion. Old Angel, having been a Primitive Methodist, had returned to the Anglican fold, though without enthusiasm. His judgment of the parson, delivered to the parson's sister, is typically East Anglian. "'That he's a po'r critter I bain't a denyin'', he would say dispassionately, 'but them as know tell ter me there ain't much chi'ce among 'em. An' ef so be as we ha'n't got much ter boast on, we must be thankful for no wuss.'"

For most of the principal characters, men and women alike, the question of allegiance to church or chapel does not arise. Yet Primitive Methodism flourished in Shropham. A chapel had been built there in the 1820's. A new and larger one was erected in 1884. There must have been a conflict in the village between church and chapel — and probably not only about religion, for where the Primitives were strong, Trade Unionists were generally active.[1] But none of the stories involves conflict between labourers and farmers: and farmers figure even less than clergymen as active characters. Here again there is a contrast between the stories and the novels, in many of which farmers are prominent. These deliberate narrowings of the subject matter to exclude the merely contemporary help to emphasise the timeless nature of the main theme: the struggle to live.

Victorian conventions of reticence were growing less strict during the 1890's when most of the stories were written — they first appeared in various magazines — though as late as 1903 Mary Mann was taken to task for including a dipsomaniac and a barmaid of doubtful virtue in "Grandma's Jane". "I defy them," she wrote to Ordish, "to find a single sentence or allusion to which the most delicate-minded could object." In the tales she easily circumvented several taboos by the use of implication. Thus, in "Women o' Dulditch", "Small wonder that Depper... preferred to the dirt, untidiness and squalor of his own abode the spick-and-span cleanliness of Dinah Brome's. Small wonder that in this

[1] This subject is given detailed treatment in A. Scotland's article, "Rural War in late Victorian Norfolk" in "Norfolk Archaeology" 1986.

atmosphere of wholesomeness and comfort he chose to spend the hours of the Sabbath during which the public-house was closed; and other hours." Or in "Old Billy Knock", where the gypsy wife had in earlier years been in the habit of visiting the pub by herself, Knock ruminates about his children: "They had tired of the land, and gone off. Healthy, brown-faced lads, as like their father as peas in a pod, his wife always assured him." In that perfectly constructed story "Levenses" she makes us feel what the return of a wife absent for eight months will mean for the husband.

Some of the tales are fashioned with great narrative skill, so that the final sentence proves essential to an appreciation of the whole — "Women o' Dulditch" is perhaps the best example. No less skill is shown in the rendering of Norfolk speech, sometimes rhymical, as when old Angel speaks of his loneliness: "Theer's jobs a man weren't never meant to 'complish in his capacity o' life; and th' time hang wonnerful heavy. I bain't a complainin', my dare wumman; for th' Lord He ha' made the sasons and the sun knoweth his a-goin' down. But my nights du fare ter'ble long now there bain't Meery no more to wait on". Mary Mann makes occasional use of dialect, as when Dinah Brome, looking through the window of Depper's cottage, sees his wretched wife crawling on all fours after spilling the uncooked cakes and realises she must help: "'I swore I wouldn't,' she said to herself as she went along, 'but I'm dinged if the sight o' Depper's old woman a-crawlin' arter them mamucked up bits o' dough ha'n't tarned my stomach'" The rendering of local speech is no easy matter. Many examples show the pitfalls of attempting too much, whether by the inclusion of too many local words and phrases or by rendering of local pronunciations which no possible combination of letters can correctly represent. In the use of the local speech she knew so well, Mary Mann strikes a perfect balance. She is the equal of such masters as Hardy and Lawrence — though there is, no doubt, some refinement, for her peasants never use an expletive!

Should the re-publication of these tales create sufficient interest in the work of Mary Mann, we hope that some of her novels may be re-published too. She was an extraordinarily prolific writer. Indeed she wrote too much too quickly because she wanted to make money regularly, at least from the time when two of her daughters needed financial support, one training to be a nurse, the other an artist. Some of the novels written before this time show strong literary ambition: "One Another's Burdens" is influenced by "Middlemarch" and "A Lost Estate" is in the mode of Hardy's tragic novels. She finds her true bent first in "The Patten Experiment" (1899) in which a group of young people, including an idealistic clergyman and his newly-married wife, attempt to live for one week in a labourer's cottage on a labourer's wage. They fail, of course, but learn salutary lessons from their experience. This novel is a social comedy in a rural setting. One senses why Thackeray had been her favourite author in scenes like that in which a clergyman's sanctimonious wife is deeply shocked.

One might name several of the interesting novels, most of them with a Norfolk setting, written between 1900 and 1910. In some of these, the labourers are portrayed with much less sympathy than in the village tales. A principal character in "Rose at Honeypot", for instance, is a lazy loutish labourer, a liar, a thief and an adulterer. Did Mary Mann, increasingly pre-occupied with her writing, no longer a young mother, lose that intimate contact with village folk she had once cultivated? Did she experience that change of manners from deference to semi-hostility which grieved the Norfolk historian Rev. Augustus Jessopp when he returned to a parson's life at Scarning? Did the best of the labourers with their families, leave Shropham, whose population fell from 433 in 1881 to 340 in 1891? However, the sourer note is subdued when Mary Mann returned to Dulditch in 1910 in one of her best novels. The title, "Astray in Arcady" may be intended as a reminder of Jessopp's splendid appraisal of Norfolk village life, "Arcady for Better for Worse". She greatly admired him. A letter to Ordish describes how, at a wedding reception she attended, the dull gathering entirely failed to appreciate Jessopp's witty and erudite speech!

"Astray in Arcady" shows her varied talents at their most lively. With that novel, "The Patten Experiment" and this collection of her tales, there would be available some good examples of one of Norfolk's finest writers.

WOMEN O' DULDITCH

DINAH BROME stood in the village shop, watching, with eyes keen to detect the slightest discrepancy in the operation, the weighing of her weekly parcels of grocery.

She was a strong, wholesome-looking woman of three- or four-and-forty, with a clean, red skin, clear eyes, dark hair, crinkling crisply beneath her sober, respectable hat. All her clothes were sober and respectable, and her whole mien. No one would have guessed from it that she had not a shred of character to her back.

The knowledge of this incontrovertible fact did not influence the demeanour of the shop-woman towards her. There was not better pay in the village, nor a more constant customer than Dinah Brome. In such circumstances, Mrs Littleproud was not the woman to throw stones.

"They tell me as how Depper's wife ain't a-goin' to get over this here sickness she've got," she said, tucking in the edges of the whitey-brown paper upon the half-pound of moist sugar taken from the scales. "The doctor, he ha'n't put a name to her illness, but 'tis one as'll carry her off, he say."

"A quarter pound o' butter," Dinah unmovedly said, "The best, please. I don't fancy none o' that that ha' got the taste o' the shop in it."

"Doctor, he put his hid in at the door this afternoon," Mrs Littleproud went on; "he'd got his monkey up, the old doctor had! ''Tis a rank shame,' he say, 'there ain't none o' these here lazy women o' Dulditch with heart enough to go to help that poor critter in her necessity,' he say."

"Ler'm help her hisself," said Mrs Brome, strong in her

indifference. "A couple o' boxes o' matches, Mrs Littleproud; and you can gi' me the odd ha'penny in clo' balls for the digestion."

"You should ha' heered 'm run on! 'Where be that Dinah Brome?' he say, 'that ha' showed herself helpful in other folks' houses.Wha's she a-doin' of, that she can't do a neighbour's part here?'"

"And you telled 'm she was a-mindin' of 'er own business, I hope?" Mrs Brome suggested, in calmest unconcern.

"I'll tell you what I did say, Dinah, bor," the shopwoman said, transferring the sticky clove-balls from their bottle to her own greasy palm. "'Dinah Brome, sir,' I say, 'is the most industrousest woman in Dulditch; arly and late,' I say, 'she's at wark; and as for her floors — you might eat off of 'em.'" She screwed the half-dozen hard red balls in their bit of paper, and stowed them lightly in the customer's basket. "That the lot this week, Dinah?"

Dinah removed her basket from counter to arm. "What'd he got to say for hisself, then?" she asked.

"'A woman like that can allust make time,' the old doctor he say. 'Tell her to make time to help this here pore sufferin' woman.' I'm a-sayin' it as he said it, Dinah. I ain't a-hintin' of it myself, bor."

"Ler'm tell me, hisself, an old interfarin' old fule, and he'll ha' the rough side o' my tongue," the customer said; and nodded an unsmiling good-afternoon, and went on her way.

Her way led her past the cottage of the woman of whom they had spoken. Depper's cottage, indeed, was the first in the row of which Dinah's was the last — a half-dozen two-roomed tenements, living-room below, bedroom above, standing with their backs to the road, from which they were divided by no garden nor even so much as a narrow path. The lower window of the two allotted to each house was about four or five feet from the ground, and was of course the window of the living-room. Mrs Brome, as she passed that of the first house in the row, suddenly yielded to the impulse to stop and look within.

A small interior, with furniture much too big for it; a huge chest of drawers, of oak with brass fittings; a broken-down couch as big as a bed, covered with a dingy shawl, a man's greatcoat, a red flannel petticoat; a table cumbered with the remains of wretched meals never cleared away, and the poor cooking utensils of impoverished, shifty housekeeping.

The woman of whom they had been speaking stood with her back to the window. A stooping, drooping skeleton of a woman, who, with weak, shaking hands, kneaded some dough in which a few currants were stuck, before laying it on a black-looking baking tin.

"A fine time o' day to bake his fourses cake!" the woman outside commented, reaching on tiptoe, the better to look in at the window.

The tin, having its complement of cakes, the sick woman essayed to carry it to the oven. But its weight was too much for her; it hung limply in her weak grasp; before the oven was reached the cakes were on the ragged carpet of the hearth.

"God in heaven!" ejaculated the woman looking in.

She watched while the poor woman within dropped on all-fours, feebly trying to gather up the cakes spreading themselves slowly over the dirty floor.

"If that don't make me sick!" said Dinah Brome to herself as she turned and went on her way.

The cottage of Dinah Brome, distant from that of Depper's wife by a score or so of yards, was, in its domestic economy, as removed from it as the North Pole from the South. Small wonder that Depper — his name was William Kittle, a fact of which the neighbourhood made no practical use, which he himself only recalled with an effort —

preferred to the dirt, untidiness and squalor of his own abode the spick-and-span cleanliness of Dinah Brome's. Small wonder that in this atmosphere of wholesomeness and comfort, he chose to spend the hours of the Sabbath during which the public-house was closed; and other hours. Small wonder, looking at the fine, capable figure of the woman, now bustling about with teapot and cups, he should esteem Mrs Brome personally above the slatternly skeleton at his own hearth.

Having made a cup of tea and cut a couple of slices of bread-and-butter, the owner of the fresh-scrubbed bricks, the fresh polished furniture, the dazzlingly white hearth, turned her back on her household gods, and, plate and cup in hands, betook herself, by way of the uneven bricked passage separating the row of houses from their rows of gardens at the back, to the house of the wife of Depper.

"I swore I wouldn't," she said to herself as she went along; "but I'm dinged if the sight o' Depper's old woman a-crawlin' arter them mamucked up bits o' dough ha'n't tarned my stomach!"

She knocked at the door with the toe of her boot, her hands being full, and receiving no answer, opened it and went in.

Depper's old woman had fallen, a miserable heap of bones and dingy clothing, upon the broken-down couch, and had fainted there.

"I'd suner 'twas anyone in the warld than you a-waitin' on me like this," she said, when, consciousness having returned during the ministrations of the other woman, her weary eyes opened upon the healthy face above her.

"And the las' time you telled me to walk out o' your house, I swore I'd never set fut in it again," Mrs Brome made answer. "But I ha' swallered worse things in my time than my own wards, I make no doubt; and you ha' come to a pass, Car'line Kittle, when you ha' got to take what you can git and be thankful."

"Pass? I ha' come to a pass, indeed!" the sick woman moaned. "You're wholly right there, bor; wholly right."

"So now you ha' got to drink this here cup o' hot tea I ha' brought ye; and let me help ye upstairs to yer bed as quick as may be."

"When I ha' baked Depper's fourses cake, and sent it off by 'Meelyer's little gal — she ha' lent her to me to go back and forth to the harvest-field, 'Meelyer have — I kin go," the wife said; "not afore," hiccoughing loudly over the tea she tried to drink; "not afore — not afore! Oh, how I wish I could bor; how I wish I could!"

"You're a-goin', this instant minute," the masterful Dinah declared.

The other had not the strength to resist. "I'm wholly done," she murmured, helplessly, "wholly done at last."

"My! How ha' you got up these here stairs alone?" Dinah, having half-dragged, half-carried the feeble creature to the top, demanded of her, wiping her own brow.

"Crawled, all-fours." Depper's wife panted out the explanation. "And to git down 'em i' the mornin's — oh, the Lord alone knows how I ha' got down 'em i' th' mornin's. Thankful I'd be to know I'd never ha' to come down 'em agin."

"You never will," said Mrs Brome.

"I don't want to trouble you, no fudder. I can fend for myself now," the poor woman said, when at length she lay at peace between the sheets; her face bathed, and the limp grimy fingers; the scant dry hair smoothed decently down the fallen temples. "I'd rather it'd ha' been another woman that had done me the sarvice, but I ain't above bein' thankful to you, for all that. All I'll ask of ye now, Dinah Brome, is that ye'll have an eye to Depper's fourses cake in th' oven, and see that 'Meelyer's gal take it and his home-brew, comf'table, to the' field for 'm."

Dinah, having folded the woman's clothes, spread them for additional warmth upon the poor bedcovering. "Don't you worrit no more about Depper," she said. "Strike me, you're the one that wants seein' to now, Car'line."

The slow tears oozed beneath Car'line's closed lids. "I kin fend for myself if Depper ain't put about," she said.

When Depper returned, with the shades of night, from the harvest-field, he might hardly have known his own living-room. The dirty rags of carpet had disappeared, the bricks were scrubbed, the dangerous-looking heap of clothing had been removed from the sofa, and a support added to its broken leg; the fireside chairs, the big chest of drawers, redolent of the turpentine with which they had been rubbed, shone in the candlelight; the kettle sang on the bars by the side of a saucepan of potatoes boiling for the meal. It was the sight of Dinah Brome at the head of affairs, however, which drew his attention from these details.

"Well, I'm jiggered!" Depper said, and paused, door in hand, on his own freshly-washed step.

"You wipe your feet, afore you come in," said Mrs Brome, masterful as ever. "Here's yer supper ready. I ain't a-goin' to ate it along of you, Depper; but I ha' got a ward or two to say to you afore I go."

Depper entered, closed the door behind him, sat down, hat on head, in the freshly-polished chair by the hearth; he fixed his eyes, his mouth fallen open, on the fine form of Dinah standing before him, with hands on hips, arms akimbo, and the masterful gleam in her eyes.

"Depper, yer old woman's a-dyin'," Dinah said.

"Marcy on us! Ye don't tell me that! Kind o' piney, like, fer the las' six months, my missus ha' bin', but —"

"Now she's a-dyin'. D'ye think I ha'n't got the right use o' my senses, arter all these years? Wheer ha' yer own eyes been? Look at 'er! No better'n a skeercrow of a woman, under yer very nose! She' a-dyin', I tell ye. And, Depper,

... with eyes keen to detect the slightest discrepancy ...

what du I come here to find? I find a bare cupboard and a bare board. Not a mite o' nouragement i' th' house, sech as a pore suff'rin' woman like Car'line's in need of."

"Car'line's a pore manager, as right well you know, Dinah. Ha'n't I telled ye —?"

"You ha' telled me — yes. But have you played th' husban's part? You ha' telled me — and I ha' put the fault o' yer poverty home on ter yer pore missus' shoulders. But since I been here, I ha' seen 'er crawlin' on 'er han's and knees to wait on you, wi' yer fourses i' th' harvest-field. I ha' heered her manderin' on, 'let things be comf'table for Depper,' and let her fend for herself. And I can see with half an eye the bute is on t'other fut, Depper. And this here is what I'm a-goin' ter say to you, and don't you make no mistake about it: I'm yer wife's woman while she wants me, and none o' yours."

Depper was a small, well-made man, with a curling, grizzled head, and a well-featured face. It is possible that in his youth the word 'dapper' may have applied to him; a forgotten fact which perhaps accounted for his nickname. He gazed with an open mouth and puzzled, blear eyes at the woman before him.

"You and me," he said slowly, with an utterance suspiciously slow and thick — "you and me ha' kep' comp'ny, so to speak, fer a sight o' years, Dinah. We never had no fallin's out, this mander, afore, as I can call ter mind. I don't rightly onderstan' what you ha' got agin me — come ter put it into wards."

"I ha' got this agin ye," the valiant Dinah said: "that you ha' nouraged yer own inside and let your misus's go empty. You ha' got too much drink aboard ye, now, an' her fit ter die for the want of a drop o' sperrits. And I ha' got this ter say: that we ha' come to a pass when I ha' got to make ch'ice twixt you and yer old woman. Arter wha's come and gone, we t'ree can't hob an nob, as ye may say, together.

My ch'ice is made, then, and this is how I ha' fixed it up. When yer day's wark is done, and you come home, I go out o' your house. Sune as ye up an' away i' th' mornin', I come in and ridd up yer missus and wait on 'er, while the woman's in need of me."

Whether this plan met with Depper's approval or not, Dinah Brome did not wait to see. "For Car'line's peace o' mind, arter wha's come and gone, 'tis th' only way," she said to herself and to him; and by it he had to abide.

It was not for many weeks. The poor unlovely wife, lying in the dismantled four-poster in the only bedroom, was too far gone to benefit by the 'nouragement' Mrs Brome contrived to administer. The sixpenn'orths of brandy Depper, too late relenting, spared from the sum he had hitherto expended on his own beer — public-house brandy, poisonous stuff, but accredited by the labouring population of Dulditch with all but magical restorative powers — for once failed in its effect. Daily more of a skeleton, hourly feebler and feebler, grew Depper's old woman; clinging, for all that, desperately to life and the hope of recovery for the sake of Depper himself.

"Let go the things of this life, lay hold on those of Eternity," the clergyman said, solemnly reproving her for her worldly state of mind. "Remember that there is no one in this world whose life is indispensable to the scheme of it. Try to think more humbly of yourself, my poor friend, less regretfully of the world you are hurrying from. Fix your eyes on the heavenly prospect. Try to join with me more heartily in the prayers for the dying."

She listened to them, making no response, with slow tears falling from shut lids to the pillow. "'Tain't for myself I'm a-pinin', 'tis for Depper," she said, the parson being gone.

"All the same, Car'line," Mrs Brome said, sharply admonishing, "I'd marmar a ward now and agin for myself, as the reverend ha' been advisin' of ye, if I was you. Depper he can look arter hisself; his time for prayin' ain't, so ter say, come yet. Yours is. I should like to hear a 'Lord help me,' now and agin from yer lips, when I tarn ye in the bed. I don't think but what yu'd be the better for it, pore critter. Your time's a-gettin' short, and 'tis best ter go resigned."

"I cud go resigned if 'tweren't for Depper," the dying woman made her moan.

"I can't think what he'll du all alone in th' house and me gone!" she often whimpered. "A man can't fend for 'isself, like a woman can. They ha'n't the know ter du it. Depper, he ain't no better'n a child about makin' the kettle bile, and sechlike. It'll go hard, me bein' put out o' th' way, wi' Depper."

"Sarve 'm right," Mrs Brome always stoically said. "He ha' been a bad man to you, Car'line. I don' know whu should speak to that if you and me don't, bor."

"He ha'n't so much as laid a finger on me since I was ill," Car'line said, making what defence for the absent man she could.

"All the same, when you're a-feelin' wholly low agin, jes' you say to yourself, "Th' Lord help me!' 'Tis only dacent, you a dyin' woman, to do it. When ye ha'n't got the strength ter say it, I'll go on my knees and say it for ye, come to that, Car'line," the notorious wrongdoer promised.

They sent for Depper to the White Hart to come home and see his wife die.

"I ain't, so ter say, narvish, bein' alone with 'er, and would as lief see the pore sufferin' critter draw her las' breath as not, but I hold 'tis dacent for man and wife to be together, come to th' finish; an' so I ha' sent for ye," Mrs Brome told him.

Depper shed as many tears over his old woman as would have been expected from the best husband in the world; and Car'line let her dying gaze rest on him with as much affection, perhaps, as if he had indeed been that ideal person.

"There'll be money a-comin' in fro' th' club," were almost her last words to him. She was speaking of the burial-club, into which she had always contrived to pay the necessary weekly pence; she knew it to be the surest consolation she could offer him.

Depper had made arrangements already for the payment of the eleven pounds from the burial-club; he had drunk a pint or two extra, daily, for the last week, the innkeeper being willing to trust him, in consideration of the expected windfall. The excitement of this handling of sudden wealth, and the dying of his wife, and the extra drink combined, completely upset his mental equilibrium. In the first moments of his widower-hood he was prostrate with emotion.

Dragged downstairs by the strong arm of Dinah Brome, he subsided into the chair on the hearth, opposite that for ever empty one of his old woman's; and with elbows on knees and head on hand he hiccoughed and moaned and wept aloud.

Above, Dinah Brome and that old woman who had a reputation in Dulditch for the laying-out of corpses, decked the poor cold body in such warmth of white flannelette, and such garniture of snipped-out frilling as, alive, Car'line Kittle could never have hoped to attain to.

These last duties achieved, Dinah descended, her arms full of blankets and pillows, no longer necessary above. These, with much banging and shaking, she spread upon the downstairs couch, indicating to the still weeping Depper it was there he was expected to pass the night.

"Bor, you may well blubber!" she said to him, with a kind of comfortable scorn of him and his sorrow. "You 'ont ketch me a-dryin' yer tears for ye, and so I tell ye flat. A crule husban' yu ha' been as any woman ever had. If ever there was a wife who was kep' short, and used hard, that was *yer* wife, Depper, my man! Bad you ha' been to her that's gone to 'er account, in all ways; who should know that better'n me, I'll ask ye? An' if at las' 'tis come home to ye, sarve ye wholly right. Tha's all the comfort ye'll get from me, bor."

"Stop along of me!" Depper cried, as, her work being finished, she moved to the door. "'Taint right as I should be left here alone; and me feelin' that low, and a'most dazed with affliction."

"Tha's how you've a right to feel," the stern woman said, unmoved by his tears.

"I keep a-thinkin' of wha's layin' up above theer, Dinah."

"Pity you di'n't think on 'er more in 'er lifetime."

"'Taint nat'ral as I should be left wholly alone with a dead woman. 'Taint a nat'ral thing, I'm a-sayin', for me to du, Dinah, ter pass the night alone along o' my old missus's corp."

"Bor, 'taint the fust onnat'ral thing you ha' done i' your life," Mrs Brome said; and went out and shut the door.

An hour or so later Depper opened it, and going hurriedly past the intervening cottages, knocked stealthily upon the door of Dinah Brome.

She looked out upon him presently from her bedroom window, her dark, crinkled hair rough from the pillow, a shawl pulled over her nightgown.

"Whu's that a-distarbin' o' me, as ha'n't had a night's rest for a week, at this time o' night?" she demanded sharply.

"It's me; Depper," the man's voice answered, whisperingly. "Le' me in, Dinah. I daren't be alone along of 'er no longer. I ha' only got you, Dinah, now my old woman's gone! Le' me in!"

"You're a rum un ter call yerself a man and a husban' — you are!" Dinah Brome ejaculated; but she came downstairs and opened her door.

OUR MARY

SHE is not indigenous to the soil of Dulditch, our Mary having been sent to us from a distant part of the country, a Heaven-given reply to our urgent need of someone to come and help us out of our muddle and take care of us.

It was the winter of our direst necessity. The rector's wife newly dead; her baby left to me, the rector's sister, a maiden lady with no knowledge of babyhood, to bring up as best I could. Guy, the other child, ill with whooping-cough; the rector himself — always an unpractical, dreary-natured man, almost paralysed by the trouble which had befallen him — nearly useless as a guide or support of his disorganised household. The servants, as is the nature of their class, deserting us in our sorest need.

She was not a person of a promising appearance — the new "general". We groaned in spirit when she first made her appearance among us — an overgrown, freckle-faced, sandy-haired girl of sixteen, wearing her best frock, a garment of green merino trimmed with black braid, far above the tops of her heavy boots; her short white apron — there were no bibs to aprons in those days and no embroidery to adorn them — standing out stiffly from a huge waist; a lace tucker in the neck of her dress and round her beef-red wrists. I look back with a smile still to Mary's advent upon the scene.

I was sitting, the baby in her wicker cradle by my side, over the dining-room fire, the nursery having been made over to Guy and his whooping-cough, when a startling knock at the door announced the new servant's arrival. To the present day our Mary insists on hammering at doors with a knuckle as hard as a poker and with a vigour that is like to splinter the panels. A rush of cold air always enters with her.

"Ef ye plase, miss, I'm come," she announced.

With a sinking of the heart I murmured that I was pleased to see her, and was going on faintly to speak to her about her future duties in the house — an oration upon which she intruded without any ceremony.

"Ye look rare and comf'table — don't ye?" she inquired.

Her pale blue eyes, with the glitter in them, roved about the room. They fell at last upon the brown wicker cradle, and with a whoop and a swoop Mary had hurled herself into the room and fallen, so to say, upon the baby.

"Well, ain't she a rare po'r little thing!" she remarked, with no consideration whatsoever for the feelings of the relatives of the infant under discussion. "Ain't she got big eyes, nayther! My mother's little Uthel, she ha' got eyes almost as blue, but they ain't so trumenjuous large!"

Upon these signs of friendly interest I asked her if she was specially fond of babies, and Mary, on her knees by the cot, looked up at me with her sidelong glance, which, darting forth from between her white lashes, has something sly and yet deprecating in it.

"I'm fond of 'em — baint't yew?" she inquired.

She had and has an incurably familiar manner; it is difficult to keep at a dignified distance from Mary.

"She be a chokin'!" she cried, looking back at the child. Her words filled me with terror. In my inexperience each fresh development of infantile ways was a cause of new alarm. "Tha's 'cos she's a laying on her back. Yew shouldn't put little uns like her on their backses."

Paying no heed to my feeble protests, she pulled the baby from the cradle. Her arms, awkward as they look, appear to have been made for the holding of children. The child, rocked in them, its little face pressed against the green frock, tight to bursting across Mary's bosom, was soon asleep, and lay peacefully on Mary's knees. She had seated herself upon the hearthrug at my feet, her own tucked under her, and she now looked critically down upon the infant, whose tiny hands she held locked in her own red fists.

"My mother's little Uthel, she 'ud make tew on her," she soliloquised. "Well, she du fare a po'r little thing! I 'spec' she bain't long for this warld," she continued; "and 'ont that be a mussy, neither, when th' Lord'll take 'er?"

I thought it less painful to decline the discussion of the baby's future, and talked to Mary instead upon what would be her duties in the house. They were duties, I took occasion to remark, with which the nursery and the children had nothing to do.

Mary gave me that sidelong glance which would so prejudice a physiognomist against her.

"When I ha' done my work I shall hold 'er though," she said, indicating the baby on her knees. "I shall ha' ter hold her, tu, I shall miss my mother's little Uthel so trumenjuous!"

We thought from former experience that the work which fell to her share would probably exhaust the "general's" energies, but we did not know our Mary. No amount of dishes to wash, of bread to bake, of floors to scrub, would keep her out of the nursery if Margaret cried, no remonstrance or entreaty or command. Nurse after nurse left on account of the "general's" unwarrantable interference. Roused to indignation at last by the resignation of a really efficient nurse, by whose experience we particularly desired the baby to profit, I gave Mary notice to quit.

Her sense of injury was great. She argued the point with me with much spirit.

"Ain't I kep' you straight and looked arter things?" she demanded. "Don't your tea and sugar last twice as long since

I'm here? Yew said it yerself. Bain't there as much again bread ate in the house since I ha' baked it? An' if so be as yew ate bread ye can't ate mate, and so your butcher's bill is seft."

I acknowledged our indebtedness to her in various ways, and commended her honesty and fidelity, but pointed out that the baby's nurse would not brook her interference.

"Yew and her want me niver so much as to touch th' baby, then?" she inquired slowly; and I confessed that that was the plain state of the case.

Mary said no more, but for a couple of days went about her work in a very half-hearted and indifferent fashion — pale of face, pink of eye and nose. At length, seeing her tears fall like rain into her wash-tub one morning, I weakly inquired into the cause of her grief.

"I miss my mother's little Uthel trumenjuous!" she said.

It has been told of me that I am always to be conquered by the sound of a snuffle — by the sight of a falling tear. I certainly succumbed on this occasion, leaving the girl triumphant, with permission to sit with the baby when her work was done, so long as she did not infringe nurse's rules.

When Guy came down from nursery regions that afternoon we learnt of fearful doings there. Over the unconscious body of the infant it seemed that the nurse and the "general" had actually fought. Nurse had thrown the baby's bottle at Mary; Mary had slapped nurse's face. Nurse had thereupon left the "general" master of the field and had gone to pack up her boxes; and almost immediately here she was at the door, very injured and angry, and insisting on leaving the Rectory at that very instant.

After that no reproaches had the effect of damping Mary's ardour.In the flush of victory she did the work of two people,and did it in such a thorough fashion as no two people at the Rectory had ever done it before. She arose before daybreak, that, her own legitimate labours being over, the coveted privilege of washing, dressing, and nursing the infant till it slept again might be hers.Hour after hour of nights when the weakly child was fretful she, untired, carried it about in her arms. In such fashion her "month's notice" crept away, and the day came on which she must go. We talked among ourselves of how she would bring herself to part from her precious charge.

"Let her stay," pleaded the rector, always tempted to do the easy thing, always yielding to pressure. I had to remind him that Mary in many things had behaved badly; that while she remained I could not uphold authority; that in the end it would be bad for Margaret. Upon which representations he turned his back, as his habit is in all controversy, and went out of the room. I had once or twice attempted a word with Mary herself on the subject of her approaching departure. She heard me in stolid silence as far as her tongue was concerned, but it must be confessed she made the plates and dishes, the kitchen doors, and the tinware to speak.

Margaret, grown a year old now, was unusually fretful on the eventful day which was to see the last of the "general". It is a humiliating fact that in spite of all my love and devoted care, my anxious desire to please, the child would always turn from my blandishments to the rough arms, the hard bosom of Mary — a curious freak of preference a little difficult to bear.

She was sitting on my lap, resisting all my efforts to amuse her, when Mary, announced by her habitual attack on the door, appeared. The "general" was attired in the green merino, grown shorter now, the black hat and white feather which on Sunday afternoons in the Rectory servants' pew were such an offence in my eyes, but which Mary had stoutly refused to relinquish. She was equipped for her journey, down to her white cotton gloves and her horn-handled umbrella.

So she stood for a minute silent in the doorway, and in

her eyes was a great scorn of my ineffectual efforts to comfort the fractious child — a great longing was in them too.

In my own eyes, somewhat to my astonishment, the tears rose. The girl had been a comfort in many ways, although so impossible in others. To be going away from Dulditch, to be leaving for ever little Margaret, was not that a fate to awake compassion in the hardest heart?

"You have been a good girl, Mary," I said. "We shall be glad to hear that you are doing well. We shall not forget you."

On Mary's part ungracious silence; on that of little Margaret loud cries and a passionate struggle to get out of my arms and to escape to Mary.

"Put 'er down and let 'er crape," Mary cried with a kind of contemptuous authority. "Yew be a hurtin' on 'er like that."

"You'll have your mother's little Ethel, you know," I reminded her, determined not to show offence, while Margaret, being put upon the floor, had hushed her crying and was putting much energy and enthusiasm into the exercise of "craping". I had hold of her dress, but she had bolted under the table, and, finding it inconvenient to follow, I perforce let her go. Running round to catch the child as she emerged, I found myself too late. With a crow of delight the little thing had made for Mary and clutched the green merino dress.

Triumphantly Mary flung down her umbrella and clawed the baby to her heart.

"I ha' got 'er," she cried with a defiant look at me. She held the child tightly with one arm and pulled off her hat and feather. "I bain't a goin' to lave her, nayther," she declared, glaring at me. "Nothin' 'ont make me lave her, and so I tell yer."

And, although this was by no means the only effort made to get rid of our Mary, she never did leave us.

"Time little Margaret live I'm agoin' to stop along of her," she always said. "When she be gone I'll go if yer like."

But although Margaret has been gone this many a year, Mary is with us still.

She is a hard-featured, middle-aged woman now, speaking always of herself as a "gal" still. She has contrived to save money in our service, the green merino having had few successors, and Mary being always "wunnerful keerful" over her things. When savings are spoken of suitors will appear, and more than once the household has been disturbed to its foundation by the announcement that its prop and mainstay was about to be wrenched from it—that our Mary was going to be married.

Experience of the worth of such intimations enables us now to treat the news with outward respect, but without any undue disturbance of equanimity.

"I ha' got another young man. I be goin' to git married, come Michaelmas," is a sentence with which we are pretty familiar.

Mary's courting exercises run about the same course, and we can watch the proceedings without any too lively an interest, knowing well what will be the end. They generally begin, as in the case of Teddy Pyman, a young man of blameless character, but of rather weak intellect, over the chickens in the spring. Mary is clever in the rearing of fowls, and in the spring of the year a good deal of her time is spent on the "drying-ground" where the hencoops are. Teddy, who makes a short cut through the small enclosed meadow on his way home from work, sits on the gate beneath the April sky and, with an abstracted air, pulls off a twig from the thorn-hedge beside him, or a gummy chestnut bud from the great tree above his head, and flings it at Mary's dress as she busies herself about the chickens. Mary, muttering to herself, with her eyes dropped to the little yellow chicks she has gathered in her apron, is as unresponsive as a stone wall. Having presently finished with the chickens, and without so much as a glance in Teddy's direction, Mary twitches some clothes off the linen line, stoops to pick up a large turnip which has fallen from a passing tumbril, and walks towards the house. The young man has slipped from the gate now, and, slouching behind her, still endeavours to attract her attention by missiles — pebbles now, or dry lumps of earth — despatched in her direction, and which hit her now and again on cheek or shoulder or in the small of her back.

Having reached the safe shelter of the kitchen door, Mary turns, and without the slightest warning responds to the above delicate attentions by flinging the turnip she carries straight in his face. The turnip is so large and she despatches it with so hearty a force that it looks like taking Teddy's head off. He is not a quick lad, but he manages to duck the ugly head in time to save it, and he greets the loud slamming of the door as Mary retreats with a yell of laughter.

When the next evening comes he is on the gate again: and the next, and the next.

Presently Mary goes out to shut up her chickens for the night without her cap. The cap is an immense improvement to Mary's appearance, but she does not recognise the fact, and always doffs it when admirers are about. Soon there comes an evening when, the grass in the drying-ground being slippery from the late rain, Mary tumbles over a refractory chicken which refuses to be tucked under its mother's wing, and measures her length upon the ground. Whereat the gallant gentleman upon the gate roars with an uncouth laughter.

"Don't set a goldering theer," Mary says, with a stiff smile upon her own long lip and a sidelong glance from beneath her white lashes. "Come and ketch it yerself, yer chump-hid!"

So encouraged, Teddy slides slowly from the gate, secures

the refractory chicken, while Mary wipes the effects of her fall from her afternoon frock; and a recognised stage in the courtship has been reached.

After this, although he makes no more effort to assist her than lies in the sticking out of a heavy foot to prevent the escape of one of the brood, or the lazy kicking towards her of the sacks with which she secures the coops from the night air, the young man always slouches at Mary's back instead of lounging on the gate, and he is reported to be "helping Mary with the chickens".

"Tha's a rare bad job he ha' got that theer cross in's eye, ain't it?" Mary inquires of me soon, by way of introducing the important subject. "That young chap — *yew* know — Tedder, then, Tedder Pyment," she explains, with the sidelong glance and the wriggle which portend the discussion of the tender passion; "I'm a kapin' comp'ny 'long o' him — him and me's goin' to git married come Michaelmas."

In Mary's preparations for marriage there is a peculiarity which I mention with diffidence, because of the censoriousness of the world. I must only entreat the charitable reader at this point not to give way to doubts which wrong her, but to hold our Mary to be, like the wife of Cæsar, above suspicion. Instead, then, of getting her *trousseau* ready, turning her thoughts to the making and laying-by of body-linen and dresses, as is the world-wide, time-honoured custom of intending brides, Mary devotes all her thought and ingenuity to the formation of the *layette*. In her bedroom she has a box devoted to her stock of baby-linen. In all her spare moments after the appearance of a lover she is to be seen busily cutting out and sewing little garments which her clumsy fingers most cleverly fashion and adorn. She mutters to herself over her needle with a very happy look.

"Ef so be as 'tis a gal — and I want it to be a gal — 'tis to be called Marg'ret," she says, displaying some of the handiwork. "Marg'ret and me used ter talk over how I were to have a little gal o' my own that were to be called arter her."

It is useless to remonstrate with her on the premature nature of her work.

"Oh, ah! Some people is allust a puttin' orf," she says with contempt.

The chance that her union might not be blessed with children has been pointed out to her.

"There bain't no sense i' getting married onless ye're to have child'en. I don't hold wi' no such a foolishness as that come tu, nayther," she says.

So for a little she stitches busily away, and then, as in the case of Teddy, the chickens being reared and Michaelmas near, a change comes over the young dream of love which periodically visits our Mary. The baby-linen is locked away in the box. Teddy may wait in vain, slouching about the kitchen door, lounging against the drying-ground gate. She takes the precaution to hang out her linen and to gather it in at an hour when the young man's occupation detains him at a safe distancc. She has no quarrel with him, enters into no argument on the subject, listens to no lover's appeal.He may linger in the autumn air amid the flapping, wet sheets, may even, urged by the desperation of his case to show the reality of his love, re-erect her linen props for her, blown down in last night's gale; or, way-laying her in an unwary moment, attempt to carry her basket of wet linen.

Without any compunction for the false hopes she has raised and the havoc she has wrought in his affections, she elbows him out of her way,tells him she has no longer time to play the fool, and gives him various salutary but blunt pieces of advice as to his future conduct.

Teddy is convinced at last that his luck is to be no better than that of his predecessors; that his chances, for that year at any rate, are over. If he stay in the same mind till the chickens come again — no newer admirer being beforehand with him on the drying-ground — he can resume his *rôle* for the season. At the end of it he will meet with the same fate.

Poor Mary! That visionary baby of hers, which was to bear the beloved name, short-coated long ago, should be old enough by now to wear the green merino in which her mother came to Dulditch. Each time that the swain is sent about his business and Mary turns to the sober duties of her life again, she presents the greater part of those shirts and gowns and flannel head-pieces to some expectant mother in the village, whose hopes are more cetainly fulfilled than Mary's. But in the spring-time, when the world that was dead, with all its hopes and promises, lives again, she is bound to set to work to fill her box once more.

While she lives, I suppose, the maternal instinct will cry out in Mary. She is so constructed that the blandishments of the rustic lover beguile her only partially and for a little while; she wearies of the "fuleries" of the mate apportioned her; but the attractiveness of that baby head which should lie against her breast, of the helpless feet that should dance in her lap, of the clinging hands in her own, will fascinate her imagination till her death-bed.

It is said in the village that Mary rules the Rectory. At the Rectory it is known that she does not rule with a gentle hand. There is an air of contemptuousness in her management of us which is a little hard to bear. We cannot always do what we will with our own: there are certain days on which we dare not invite visitors to our house; there are one or two parishioners to whom we have to show attention *sub rosa,* Mary not approving of their persons or characters or ways of "goin' on"; there are others who are pushed forward for soup and brandy and "pieces" on all occasions. There was one summer-time, she being for some reason unusually crusty ("short-waisted" she calls this state of mind herself), when she would not sanction our giving the annual school treat. We dared not undertake it without her approval.

She is always specially "difficult" when the church bells ring; can barely tolerate their tolling for church, and is rendered furious by the practice for Christmas, the New Year, and other festivals. She has, indeed, a curious terror of music. It is not often now that there are any to make music at the Rectory, but on those occasions when Guy runs down, and old friends of his look in upon us; when the piano is opened again, and again the

> "Plaintive numbers flow
> For old unhappy, far-off things,
> And battles long ago,"

then Mary takes refuge in the underground cellar and muffles her head in a shawl.

It may be that the "melancholy madness" is trying to Mary's nerve; it may be that she is unusually susceptible of the charm of music; she is, perhaps, dimly conscious that, if she ceased to withstand its sway, its power over her might become irresistible; perhaps the "measured malice" awakes within her longings which tear her breast with unspeakable pain. Mary does not plead any of these excuses. She calls music a "terrufic n'ise," and says it gives her a "sinkin' in 'er in'ards."

She might be induced to go to the church oftener but for the music, she thinks, but she speaks with no certainty on the point. Familiarity, I fear, has accomplished its usual office, and bred contempt in the Rectory servant of the forms of that religion which is the Rectory "consarn," as she puts it. She is unable to separate the master in the pulpit, with his learning, his ascendency, his voice of authority, from the master of the home, who has to be scolded for forgetting to put a comforter round his neck; whose study fire has to be lit six times a day because he is not to be trusted o put on the coals; who is so wickedly unpunctual about neals.

"I don't want him a-setting up ter tache me," Mary says with frank disdain; "ef so be as ivver I want ter pray, I take it I kin pray without such as him."

So, instead of going to church, Mary sits over the kitchen fire on the Sabbath with her Bible in her lap. It is, in fact, a monster Bible, being one which she bought at the door of a travelling agent, expending all her earnings upon it — long ago, when Margaret was a baby.

There never was a Sunday afternoon after the acquisition of this treasure which Mary and Margaret did not spend over its vilely illuminated sheets. The tiny fingers could point out Noah on his knees before his fire of sticks, the rainbow over his head, Abraham with the abnormal muscular developments, the sacrificial knife raised above his son, long before her baby tongue could speak their names. On the very last Sunday afternoon of the child's life she and Mary went through the pages with as much interest as if they had never seen them before.

On that day, coming home from church, I entered the Rectory by the kitchen door. The kitchen had that inexplicable, indescribably Sabbath air which places have on the hallowed day, which Nature herself always wears. On the much-scrubbed deal table was a great brown gotch full of lilac, and the Bible, with Margaret, her head propped on her hand, leaning over it; one of Mary's hard red hands rested on the book waiting to turn the leaves. (She always honours the Sabbath day by wearing in the afternoons a brass watch-chain which one of her lovers gave her.) I remember that Margaret's brown hair, turned to bronze and gold in places by the kiss of the afternoon sun, fell upon the picture of the Flood.

It is partly the possession of that enormous Bible which gives Mary such a feeling of superiority to the rector. Once, in a moment of expansion, anxious to share the blessings that were hers, she carried the book, wrapped in the cloth which always enveloped it, into the dining-room and laid it proudly down before her master's chair.

"The gays are wonnerful instructin'," she said, her eyes on her treasure, her person modestly withdrawn from its neighbourhood. "There's in ut Angels, and Balum's dicky a crunching of his master's fut."

The rector, who does not care to tackle Mary herself, was very severe when her back was turned on the sin of vulgarising Holy Writ by such abominable caricatures. As he turned from one illustration to another he grew reproachful as well as severe. Surely, he said, we who for so many years had enjoyed the inestimable privilege of sheltering this good and faithful servant beneath our roof should have done something to correct her taste, to elevate her understanding. She had given us her best, and we — what had we done in return? The duties we felt called upon to perform towards our inferiors were only gross, material ones. If we had fed sumptuously, knowing that one among us was perishing for want of food, we should be called culpable, and the world would cry out on us. But here was one, starved of all culture, associating with us who boasted of our refinement, yet a savage in matters of taste. "Shame! Shame!" said the rector, having turned his back on the book, and mildly lecturing his son and me as he paced the room.

And then Guy, who happened to be at home on that occasion, and who had lounged up to inspect the cause of so much eloquence, gave a shout of laughter and called on his father to admire with him the representation of Lot's wife.

And while the Rector, his homily forgotten, an unwilling smile on his lips, stood there with a hand upon Guy's shoulder, I took heart to tell him how, for all her little life, Margaret had loved the blue and red and yellow daubs; and I told him too of that picture, always present to my mind, of the child on that last Sunday afternoon with her rippled hair falling upon the picture of the Flood.

After that the rector sat down by Guy's side, and silently and in reverence looked at the dreadful plates, and said no other word of condemnation. And presently, when the end was reached, he arose and himself carried back the book into the kitchen. Then, in that polite and deferential manner he always exhibits to Mary, he thanked her for her kindness in lending the book and for all her kindness.

"I don't want ter fluster myself to go to church now I ha' got that, do I now?" Mary calls after him, gratified and triumphant, as he departs. The rector hastens his steps a little; he always shirks an argument with Mary.

"So long as I ha' got 'em all theer, and kin see th' devil a temptin' o' Ave, and th' 'arth a-opinin' ter swaller Abiram, I bain't a-goin' ter trouble no fudder about 'em," Mary mutters to herself, turning back to her book.

A DULDITCH ANGEL

"SHE lived by my side a matter o' sixty yare, and she niver so much as laid a straw i' my path," said old Angel to me, speaking of the wife he had just buried.

He was a little old man, blue-eyed, white-haired, apple-cheeked. He was dressed in the Sunday suit which had distinguished him, perhaps, from the time when he went courting the paragon he lamented: a long worn velveteen coat adorned with brass buttons, a tall hat, decorated with a hat-band now, worn at the back of his head. Under one arm he carried a huge green umbrella, under the other a heavy stick. Outside his own gate he never ventured without these implements of offence and defence; he brought both to church as regularly as he brought his Bible and Prayer-book. I never remember to have seen him use either.

There may have been in former years weather "big" enough to warrant him in mounting the green umbrella, but he speaks of present-day downfalls cheerfully as "a m'isture," and lets the rain beat upon his round, rosy face, and pour off the battered brim of his tall hat, keeping his gingham safely under his arm the while. Perhaps he shrinks from seeming to claim a superiority over the other men, who have no spare cash for such trivialities as umbrellas, and who adopt no protection from the storm other than an old artificial manure sack flung over their shoulders. Perhaps he fears lest the rain should injure the dear possession. It is never unfolded, neither is his stick used for support.

Old Angel lived at the extremity of the parish in a little one-storied cottage, planted all alone behind a long strip of garden, where marigolds and the dark columbine, tall white lilies, and the old York and Lancaster rose grew among the gooseberry and currant bushes. For Angel was, as will be seen, a man of sentiment and encouraged the beautiful.

The garden boasted also a very old greengage tree, the pride of old Angel's heart.

With his umbrella and his stick tucked away under his arms, he would toddle up to the Rectory in the early spring to solicit orders for the fruit. It was an unceasing satisfaction to him — a satisfaction, however, which he politely strove to conceal — that there was not a greengage tree in all the Rectory garden.

"I thought as how I'd be betimes wi' ye for th' gages," he would say; "I thought as how I'd give ye fust chancet. I ha' heared tell as th' Rev'rend is agraable to th' fruit; and I think, ef so be as my mem'ry don't mislade me, ye ha'nt a gage i' yer orn gaarden?"

We always hastened to confirm this point and to lament the fact.

"Maybe 'tis made up to ye," he would continue, as one who was loath to press an advantage. "Theer be a fine bully" (bullace tree) "I know i' th' orchard; for one day we was a-talkin' matters over, th' Rev'rend and me, and he telled me so hisself. He di'nt patronomise th' bully like th' gages, from what he let onto me. Howsever, there be a good show t' year — th' tree be a picter for blow, and ef so be as th' kerstels" (clusters) "set, yer may reckon I'll be able to 'blige ye. An' ef so be as I kin, my dear wumman, you may be sure I wull."

The time of blossom is the only time of triumph for old Angel, for the harvest of the tree is apt to be sadly disappointing. We at the Rectory have had to make up to him for the deficiency of the measure we had ordered by unmeasured praise of the quality of the fruit.

"'Tis a good gage," the old fellow would admit dispassionately, looking mournfully upon the pint or so of the plums — the entire crop — he was transferring from his basket to our own, "and th' Rev'rend is agraable to th' fruit, I know. The bully be a useful sorter plum, but he ain't to comparison in tastiness to th' gage."

The tears ran down his cheeks as he talked about the old wife he had just laid in the churchyard. It was of her goodness to him alone he spoke; but for years we in Dulditch had witnessed his patience, his tenderness, his unfailing devotion to the peevish and afflicted old woman whose loss he now artlessly mourned.

She was, it had seemed to us, a troublesome, unlovable patient, fractious, ungrateful, indocile. In the last years of her life she had been imbecile as well as incurably afflicted in other ways. As gently and as wisely as a good mother waits on her stricken child did the old husband wait upon his wife. There were no near neighbours, and those from a distance who had lent a helping hand soon tired of the unremunerative office. He made no protest or complaint; cheerfully and alone he laboured on.

A young man rejoices over his bride, wondering at her beauty, waiting on her whims, indulging her caprices, worshipping her with heart and eye; and the world smiles indulgent at the pretty sight. Over such a devotion as this of the ignorant old pauper husband to his unlovely, ungracious old wife it has seemed to me that the angels themselves might smile, well pleased.

"I'll tell ye how't be," he said, with his little half-childish chuckle, one day when I had been moved to express to him my appreciation of his untiring care and tenderness; "I'll tell ye th' wuds I used ter say ter my old wumman in our young time, when her and me, happen, di'n't allust think alike, as, happen, men and wummen sometimes don't,

'Meery' I'd say, 'Meery,' (these hare be th' wuds), 'theer's on'y one thing to be put down to yar favour, Meery, bor,' I'd say, 'and that be — I love yer.'"

He nodded his head triumphantly at this reminiscence. "Tha's how't be, ye see, wi' Meery and me," he cried in concluding the matter — "Tha's how't be."

About his poverty, any more than about his trials with his invalid wife, he never complained. He was neither ungrateful for kindness nor avaricious of benefits. He was incapable of grudging what fell to another's share or was given to another's necessity. More than once he refused the little money-help that could be offered him.

"Kape it yerself, my dare wumman," he said, his stiff fingers closing mine upon the coin in my hand. "Ye'll maybe want it as much as me. I ha' heered tell as how money's skeerse up to th' Rect'ry, and th' Rev'rend he don't look no matters hisself. Come sickness, tha's expensive, as ye'll find, mayhap. Kape 't yerself and thenk 'e."

For any little service he does accept, the white lilies, and red and white striped roses of his garden pay a pretty toll. So sure as a can of broth, a medicine-bottle filled with wine, is despatched to him, so surely does old Angel present himself with the floral tribute gathered from among the gooseberry bushes. In payment for the old night-shirt from the Rector's stock, given him to be buried in, he insisted on bequeathing me the lavender-bush from beside his door.

The last garment which shall drape their mortal bodies is always a matter of serious import to the poor. It was with much reluctance that old Angel confided to me the fact that the shirt which had been set aside for his own burial had been taken to deck the body of his wife; she, during the irresponsible condition of the last few years of her life, having "made a hand o' th' shift" she had provided for the occasion.

The lavender-bush was especially precious to her husband, as "Meery" had set it and had always "favoured" the plant. He had "strowed" her body with the flowers when she lay in her coffin, he told me.

Angel had been born and bred a Primitive Methodist, but seceded from that body twenty years or so before his death and came over to the Church, the reason he gave being that he wished to "set under" a gentleman.

"Why, him as prache at chapel bain't no better nor me," he used to say, with fine contempt. "Wha's th' good o' his settin' hisself up ter mandate ter me. Gi' me a preacher as kin look down on yer, high and haughty-like, to hold forth. I don't, so to say, set no store by none o' them smiley and similiar" (familiar) "ones."

He was an out-and-out Conservative, although he never knew it, and was always on the side of the moneyed classes and of authority.

"Them as ha' th' proputty is them as oughter rule," he said. "'Tis for th' quality to ha' th' haughtiness, and for we to ha' th' manners. Manners don't cost nowt, as I tell 'em, and a man'll be a sight o' time a-wearin' up 's hat by touchin' on it. As fur a-settin' up ter be akal" (equal) "alonger th' gentry and sech like — why 't can't niver be done — niver! Theer be them, sure enow, and hare be we, and us can't imitate ter say as we be o' th' same pattern. Why, even in heaven, bless th'Lord, theer be the angels and the archangels, and ef so be as I ha' to chuse when I git theer, I think, hapen, 't'll be th' lessest o' th' two I make ch'ice on."

Such views would not meet with approval in the "White Hart" sanded kitchen, or even in Littleproud's shop, but old Angel was not a frequenter of either place.

He was one of the rector's staunchest upholders, although his favourite form of defence, when put down in black and white, appears somewhat of the lukewarm order, and his praise seems to some of us unnecessarily faint.

"That he's a p'or critter I bain't a denyin'," he would say

dispassionately, "but them as know tell ter me there ain't much chi'ce among 'em. An' ef so be as we ha'n't got much ter boast on, we must be thankful for no wuss. Th' Rev'rend — yew kin see he've got book-larnin', by the wacant look on 'im, and I'm one for heerin' them as ha' book-larnin' hold forth. Ef so be as yew ha'n't th' ondeerstandin' for't — 'tis wallable all th' same. I ha'n't naught to say agin th' Rev'rend, considerin' his capacity o' life."

It is said that the greatest compliment a man can pay his wife is to take another after her death. The number of wives who wish to have the admiration of their husbands so expressed is probably small. Be that as it may, it is certain that old Angel, who had loved and sincerely mourned his mate, lost no time in trying to replace her. He was specially attracted to our own faithful and invaluable domestic through the coincidence of her bearing the Christian name of the deceased Mrs. Angel. On the day that he called to arrange with the rector the hour for the burying he made an offer of himself, hand and heart, stick, umbrella, and two-and-sixpence a week, to our Mary while he waited in the kitchen.

We were a little shocked at such precipitancy, but we soon learnt that even this was not his first *affaire,* he having already proposed matrimony to Susannah Chaney, the widow woman who had been summoned to lay Mary Angel forth.

Our Mary always refused to believe that she herself was not the widower's first choice, and she stoutly discredited Mrs. Chaney's report. For although Mary had treated the old man's proposal with the savagest contempt, the report that another had seen fit to refuse him filled her with fury.

"Oh, dessay!" she said with fine disdain, and dashing the crockery about, as is her reprehensible habit when her temper is disturbed. "Refuged on 'm, have she? Oh, dessay! What Sesanner! Ketch 'er at it!"

But Mary's anger could not alter facts, and the fact is well authenticated that within the six weeks following his wife's death old Angel made as many as a dozen offers of marriage. Among women of all ages, from eighteen years to eighty, he sought a mate, and I, for my part, think it a great pity he could not find one. He was a cheerful, chirpy, companionable little old man, and he found his solitary fate very hard to bear. In marrying I believe that he was chiefly anxious to find a companion to whom he might chatter incessantly of the defunct Mary. He had treasured up in his mind, to produce on the shortest notice, a store of the perfectly pointless remarks to which she, in the sixty years of their married life, had given utterance, and of the entirely unremarkable replies they had called forth. But the attitude of the peasant mind is not critical; it is only the oft-told tale that finds favour, and there always seems to be a preference for the one that has neither end, nor beginning, nor life, nor favour. I do not think that the second Mrs. Angel, if she had ever existed, would have understood that she should have been bored to death by such reminiscences.

His cottage stood away by itself in a very lonely part of Dulditch, quite half a mile from any other habitation. Unless the old man shouldered stick and umbrella and came "up-town way" in search of society, he might go for weeks without seeing a soul to speak to. He had grown so old as to be very much a child again in many ways, and he had a child's fear of being alone.

Interminable those long summer days must have semed to him, no particular work falling to his hand to do. The gooseberries and currants picked, the pea- and bean-stalks — their produce all gathered and eaten — pulled up, the garden — for the greater part laid out in rows of potatoes — required just now no attention. But the habit of a lifetime cannot be abandoned when there is no longer any call for its performance, and old Angel still arose when the day was in its earliest hazy freshness. Hours before it was time for his breakfast he had completed those small household jobs which were all he had to look forward to for the day's occupation. From the time he broke his fast — from eight o'clock in the morning till eight at night, when he locked his house door and went to bed — time must have hung wearily on his hands. How he lingered over taking up the one root of potatoes which yielded enough for his dinner! What a business he made of washing, and peeling, and putting in the pot! After that there was only to watch the potatoes boil, and to turn them bodily into the big yellow basin in the centre of the table — the basin which for sixty years had been wont to hold a double share.

He ate his portion with tears now, and many gurgling noises, and little clicks of emotion, but having eaten invariably felt strong and perky again, and would place his tall hat on his little white head — he always wore the rector's left-off hats, which were sizes too large for him — and saunter jauntily down to the garden gate to look out for moving incidents of the road, and to intercept the passer-by.

He made a practice of hailing all the carts that passed by means of his uplifted stick. Now and again a driver would obey the summons and would let his pony crop the grass by the roadside, or pull at the long branches of the honeysuckle and blackberry bramble trailing over the fence, while he exchanged a word or two on the state of the weather and the crops with the lonely old man. On rare occasions the present of a lettuce for his tea, or some sticks of rhubarb for his "old woman to put down", would tempt a passer-by to enter the gate, to wander down the narrow garden path, bounded by the currant and gooseberry bushes, to stand and stare with old Angel at the "inion" bed, to contemplate the long rows of potatoes, and to hear the history of every row — which went in at the time observed by universal custom, and which was the result of the wild experiment of "Febbiwary plantin'."

The days that the old man toddled down to report himself to the relieving officer and to receive his dole of money and of bread were red-letter days in his calendar. Waiting about among the old widows collected for the same purpose, he offered himself wildly, right and left, in matrimony, as did that gallant knight Sir John Dureley in days of yore at Windsor.

"'Tain't good for man to be alone," he reminded me when I spoke to him on the subject. "Theer's jobs a man weren't never meant to 'complish in his capacity o' life; and th' time hang wonnderful heavy. I bain't a complainin', my dare wumman; for th' Lord He ha' made th' sasons, and the sun knoweth his a'goin' down. But my nights du fare ter'ble long now there bain't Meery no more to wait on."

I noticed that he had aged a great deal in a very little time, and that his cheerful perkiness had ceased to be a habit and was only assumed on occasion.

One morning he appeared at the Rectory carrying a little parcel tied in a cabbage leaf, as well as the umbrella and stick beneath his arm.

"I thought, happen, I'd make sure as yer had yer bush," he said as he untied the string of this parcel; "there's no accouontin' for how matters 'll be at th' gaarden arter I'm gone. Th' incomer he, mayhap, 'll want ter stick ter th' lavender. As long as Meery planted on't I don't fare i' the' mind to dig it up — not i' my time. Tha's where she wushed th' bush ter be, stan' ter rayson, else why'd th' wumman plant it theer? An' ef so be as Meery bain't hare to spake fur 'erself, I don't keer to cross her wushes, that laid alongside o' me fur sixty yare. So I ha' tuk slips o' th' bush, and I think y'll stan' a chancet o' raisin' on 'em. And ef so be as my time's come, I kin fare aisy ye ha'n't been chated out o' yer lavender."

He said, in answer to inquiry, that he was feeling "no

matters" that morning, and that he fancied "mayhap" the Lord had need of him, and that his time was about come. "My po'r Meery, she be gone," he sighed, wiping the back of his little horny red hand across mouth and nose, "and I reckon as I'm ter foller."

He had caught a "chronic cold" the night before, he said, "t'rough slapin' wi' th' windy open." Reminded that the heat of the summer was over and that the year had suddenly turned very cold, he admitted his imprudence.

"'Twere th' furst frost o' th' yare," he acknowledged sadly. "Th' daylies i' Littleproud's gaarden be all black and limpsy-laved this mornin', and the mar'go's and snapdragons is dead. 'Twere strikin' cold. But theer was raysons," he added mysteriously, with a bewildered trouble in his moist blue eyes. Touching me confidentially on the arm, he repeated the phrase in a whisper: "Theer was raysons, my dare wumman, why I ope'd the windy."

He went away carrying the "chronic" cold and the familiar stick and umbrella, and I thought that the little old man looked smaller than ever — strangely shrunken and dwindled.

It was Amelia Sprite, the woman who once a week "rid th' old chap up," who a few days later volunteered to enlighten me on the subject of the "raysons". Amelia is a gossiping, foolish woman, not at all a favourite of mine. She hailed me as I hurried past her door — her manner is always entirely wanting in respectfulness. I find it advisable to avoid conversation with her as much as possible.

"Ye've heerd as po'r old man Angel is harnted?" she called. "He be, howsomdever, sure enough," she added with curt insistence when I indignantly repudiated the notion. "'Tis old Meery a worritin' on 'm again, most like. She allust were a onsat'sfied, restless old critter. I take it more'n likelies she 'ont lay quiet i' th' graveyaard."

Amelia treated my angrily remonstrant remarks as if she

had not heard them.

"She be allust a flappin' across 's faace sure as th' dark come on and he crape into 's bed," she continued. "Th' po'r old chap, he's all on a trimble when's time come ter lay down. I ha' left 'm of a muck-swat when I ha' closed th' door on 'm. 'Tis old Meery, sure 's eggs; I tell'd 'm so from th' fust; and he don't imitate ter deny as how 't be."

I tried to point out to Amelia the wickedness of putting such ideas into the head of old Angel, who had been so good to his wife and who still so loved her memory.

"He bain't so fond o' havin' on 'er floppin' about over 's faace for all that, I kin tell yer," Amelia called after me defiantly, as I walked indignantly away.

There is no real harm in the woman, only she is made so that she must "run on," the neighbours say. She has worked much mischief by her ignorant tongue. Her "running on" in the present case had certainly a disastrous result.

The old man sat and shivered over his fire; all the cheerfulness gone out of him for ever; a stricken look on his face. He received all that was said to him deferentially and did not attempt any argument, but it was easy to see that his belief in the supernaturalness of his experience was not shaken.

"'Tain't till I'm abed and th' light out," he said dejectedly, "then she begin a whirrin' and a swoopin' and a flappin'."

"Why do you call it — this thing of your imagination — she?"

The watery blue eyes were shifted from mine, and he did not answer.

"Oh, Angel! You that spoke to me with such beautiful faith of the heavenly home to which your wife had gone!"

He gave the hand that was laid on his a trembling pressure.

"Maybe I was i' tew much 'f a hurry," he said timidly.

"Maybe she weren't gone so much 'f a suddint. Mayhap she be a waitin' fur me!"

"Don't lie in darkness. Keep your candle burning for to-night."

He evidently thought me crazy to make such a suggestion.

"My dare wumman, 'twould gutter down 'n a jiffy in th' draught from th' open windy."

"Shut your window. Your bed is directly beneath it —you might as well lie in the open air."

"I kape 'i open agin she may take 'i in 'er hed to go out by the windy," he explained. "I lave th' sneck o' th' door undone for th' same rayson."

Small wonder he had a cold, small wonder the "rattlin'" on his chest was, as he said, "terrufic"!

"Put out your hand and catch the thing," I counselled him. "It is either a bird or it is nothing. I incline to think it is a bird."

"'Tain't naything," he said with resigned wretchedness. "'Tis a sight tew big for ayther o' them. 'Tis my po'r Meery herself, I make no doubt."

"'Tis a bat," our Guy said, laughing, when he heard the tale.

"A bat! My dear Guy, he describes a thing of as much size and importance as an eagle. He couldn't possibly have mistaken anything like a bat for his Mary!"

"Ten to one 'tis a bat," Guy persisted. The boy is very fond of his own opinions. He is bound to be, as they are always right, he says. "'Tis a bat that hides in some corner in the daytime and flies about at night. Be sure you tell him 'tis a bat, sir," he said to his father, who was standing hat in hand ready to depart, in obedience to a wish old Angel had expressed to see "th' Rev'rend" and to take the sacrament.

The rector forgot the pocket communion service and presently came back for it. Five minutes later we heard his step in the hall again, and Mary put her head in at the door to tell us that the master could not remember if it was old Angel who wished to communicate, or Martha Brown's brother (commonly called among us Fitz-Brown because he is subject to fits), who was lying ill of a "twinsy" at the other end of the parish.

"The dear old shepherd!" Guy said, laughing a little sadly as he watched the bent figure of my brother disappearing for the third time through the Rectory gate; "he is always so sadly 'mixed' about his sheep."

When I lay down in my own comfortable bed that night and put out the light, my thoughts wandered to old Angel at the far end of the village. The solitary old man, ill, and haunted by his ignorant fears! By dwelling on them, his loneliness and his terror oppressed me. The night was inky black, a dreary length of uninhabited road and a thick plantation of dark firs, full of melancholy noises and ugly possibilities, separated him from any human help. The wind was abroad, I heard it sweeping through the trees in the garden; it came tearing round the corner of the house; the blind over my window stirred and rustled; a creeper tapped, like a peremptory finger, against the pane; I began to feel old Angel's terror as a very real thing.

"Put out your hand and lay hold of whatever it is that hovers over your face," I had said; I who cannot repress a shudder if an "arwriggle," as Mary calls an earwig, crawls upon my dress, and who screamed aloud the other evening when a midsummer daw dashed itself in the dark against my face. Dare I, twenty years younger than the feeble old man, nurtured in no superstitious terrors, strong of body and fairly sane — dare I put out my hand in the dark and grasp at any felt but unseen, mysterious presence?

How terrible, when one's mind dwells on them, are the sufferings of the poor! How horrible, above all, is the enforced solitariness of the very old! To be ill and quite alone; in terror — terror of an exaggerated kind it must have been, which could have reduced cheery, pleasant old Angel to his present physical condition, and put that look of trouble in his serene blue eyes — quite alone; thirsty — as the human soul must always be for sympathy, companionship, comfort — longing for the touch of a friendly hand, the sound of a friendly voice — always alone!

Something might have been done for him if I had realised all this quite in the same way before. I might have induced old Skipper, his rheumatics being temporarily better, to hobble down on his crutches and share the horrors of the night with the other old man. Skipper was a soldier once, and is reported to be afraid of nothing. Perhaps "Dummy" Borrett, who, being stone deaf, can't have been frightened by the story of the "harntin'," would, for a consideration, have sat at the bedside.

As it was, I pictured the old blue and white checked curtains of the four-poster swaying in the night wind, the poor shivering figure upon the bed, cowering, waiting for that mysterious swirling of the air which would come surely at last, that swoop of something huge, shadowy, awful across his face. The poor defenceless, kindly old man, suffering the agonies of a terror which nothing earthly, surely, could call forth. The unseen presence is lifted. There comes another rush through the air, another swirl and swoop, nearer to his face this time.

My own hair had begun to creep with horror. I kindled the light again and took up a Book which lies always by my bedside, wherewith to exorcise the spirit of terror.

The next day happened to be that of the weekly "redding-up", at which Amelia Sprite officiated. The gale of the previous night was still blowing when "Meelyer" reached the old man's cottage. The door, "unsnecked" for the egress of "Meery", was blowing noisily to and fro; the blue and white cotton curtains of the four-poster were tossing wildly in the wind from the wide-open lattice. Old Angel was lying upon the bed, still and dead.

The toothless mouth, the one visible eye, were wide open, giving a look of terror to the face. Over the other eye and over part of the sunken cheek something black was lying, which on closer inspection proved to be a bat.

Before she discovered the nature of the object, Meelyer, with the touch of disgust, had twitched the shrivelled-looking patch off the face. For a moment or two it fluttered feebly on the floor till Meelyer's heavy foot put an end to its existence.

Guy had been right as usual. "Did you tell the poor old fellow his ghost was only a bat, sir?" he asked of his father.

But the rector had forgotten. A circumstance the more curious as he now recalled the fact that while reading and praying with old Angel he had observed a bat clinging to the top of the bed among the curtains.

"Bat or no bat, 'twere Meery," Meelyer Sprite said. "'Twere old Meery, safe enough. And I jemmed my fut on 'er, thank th' Lord."

RATS!

ALICK is digging the rose-bed in the Old Master's garden. The duties of Alick are multifarious. He cleans the knives and boots, fills the coal-hods, feeds the pigs, helps in the stable, pumps the water for the maids. He is nineteen years of age, and receives a stipend of eight shillings a week. He is of a rather torpid disposition, but there is in his mind a lively anxiety so to order the performance of his services that they should not be worth more to his employers than the sum paid for them. He is tall, with hard-shining, expressionless eyes, and an ever-open mouth.

His attention is very easily diverted from the work in hand; and as he slowly drives his spade into the heavy earth of the half-dug rose-bed, it is attracted by a little group of young men and maidens passing through the gardens —girls, sportsman-like and trim, in skirts short to the ankle, tweed hats, golf coats; men in breeches and belted jackets; one of them holds a bag in his hand, one carries a gun upon his shoulder; a couple of little fox-terriers are at their heels. Perceiving the youth with the spade to be staring at them with his glassy eyes, they stop, and explain to him that they are there by permission of the Old Master for a morning's ratting on his premises.

"You've got a quantity of rats about, in these old stacks and buildings, I suppose?" one of the party says to him.

"Dessay," says Alick, applying the back of his hand to his nose, and staring ahead.

"Can you show us where they principally lie?"

"No."

"You can't?"

"They're all abeaout."

"But mostly in the stables, cow-houses, granaries?"

"Mostly i' th' hidges," Alick vouchsafes. "The banks down the Sandy Lane's raddled with 'em."

"Really! And where is Sandy Lane, then?"

"Acrost theer!" If Alick's eyes could have been eloquent of anything, it would surely have been of a surprised contempt for a person who did not know the whereabouts of Sandy Lane! "T'rough th' clover layer and the turmit field, and athwart th' ploughed land, and a corner o' Widder's Midder."

"Widow's Meadow? That's interesting. Why is it called Widow's Meadow?"

Alick, who accepted his facts and never troubled about the whys and wherefores of more curious minds, simply stared.

"You think we should have more luck in Sandy Lane than in the stackyard, for instance? The Old Master said something about the piggeries —"

"Theer might be a chancet one, here and theer; but i' th' Sandy Lane theer's a sight of 'em."

"Bring your spade and come with us."

But he had his "wark ter du," Alick said, and struck his spade in the earth with great force to show that he was no trifler. Having got so far, however, he paused, and, great foot on spade, watched the retreating party making for Sandy Lane. He did not smile to himself, nor sigh, not give vent to any sentiment he might have had in regard to them; he simply looked, with vacant stare and lopping mouth, till he could see them no more, then spat upon his hands and went on slowly digging.

The party of young people had a very pleasant morning in Sandy Lane, which they worked in business-like fashion from end to end. They did not get on to any rats, but were not perhaps the less happy. The youngest girl, who wore her hair still in tails, had a secret terror of seeing one killed, and preferred to watch the wriggling undulations of the ferrets safe within their bag in her brother's hand to seeing them disappear into holes, where you never knew what might happen! The elder ladies, armed with murderous sticks, were quite ready to give account of any rats which ran in their direction. But then, the young men who handled the ferrets and carried the guns were not *their* brothers, and ratting was not the only sport they had come out to play.

The brown ploughed lands and forsaken harvest fields lay serene that morning beneath a sun robbed of his power to torment. The air was kind and the heavens azure. The scant leaves of the beech, the elm, the oak, golden and lemon-coloured and bronze against the blue, detached themselves regretfully from the parent branch and silently floated down to join the majority lying moist and shining on the roadside grass.

The little group of young people sat to eat their lunch on the light soil of the bank beneath the Scotch firs; and they decided that November was the rippingest month of the year in which to have a meal out-of-doors. How jolly the coral-red berries were in the hedges —jollier even than the jolly little roses had been. How simply too sweet was the plaintive note of the chaffinch, and the "chittering" of the little birds in the thorn. A robin, hopping ever nearer, bore them company while they stayed, and in the finish they stilled their laughing and chatter in order not to abash him when he came to their feet to pick up the crumbs they tossed him.

And when the air had grown more chill, and the light of the short afternoon had begun to fade from the sky, in an old thatched bullock shelter which they passed on their way home, they did have the satisfaction of killing a rat.

They held it up to Alick in his rose-bed as they passed him, going through the garden.

"We didn't see *one* in your Sandy Lane," they called to him.

"Mayhap you skeered 'em away," Alick suggested; and growled after them the information already vouchsafed, that the banks was raddled with 'em.

Then he withdrew his spade, wiped it, and walked away, for his day's work was done.

But before he betook himself homeward, he repaired to a certain building, a sort of antechamber to the piggeries, where stood a huge open boiler in which meal was mixed for the pigs. The place was already in darkness, and, as Alick opened the door, letting in a tempered light, there was a hurry and a scuttle, and forms shadowy and noisome sprang from the brim of the boiler and disappeared; and something secret and loathly ran over Alick's boots.

To the sides of the copper remnants of the pigs' last meal were hanging. Having dislodged these portions and massed them at the bottom, Alick withdrew the stick which had served as escape-ladder for the rats he had disturbed, and went on his way to home and supper.

In the morning he arose an hour before his usual time, and made his way to the same building, lantern in hand.

In that receptacle which had held the pigs' meal, and from which all means of egress had been taken, what a struggling, seething mass of noxious vermin was there! What a noise of scratching upon the smooth sides, of scrabbling, scrambling, squeaking, shrieking! Into what a miniature inferno was the copper converted!

Alick set his lantern where its dim light could fall upon that ugly, writhing mass, and gazed into the pit of destruction with staring, expressionless eyes and lopping mouth. Then he fetched a heavily knobbed stick he had procured for the purpose, and set to work.

Alick was not at all interested in the great war of rat-extermination raging in his native county; he had not even heard of the bubonic plague; but he had been told on the previous day that a prize of a penny had been offered for every rat murdered on the premises. And when the Old Master had finished his breakfast, and was ready to sally forth upon his leisurely rounds that morning, he was waylaid by Alick, who proceeded to drag from his pockets the blood-stained trophy of one hundred and seven rats tails, for which he demanded immediate payment.

BEN PITCHER'S ELLY

HAIR as golden as sunlit corn; a skin of roses — red and white; eyes blue like the May-day sky, bright and clear and sweet — Ben Pitcher's Elly.

So attractive-looking and winning a child was she that some in Dulditch were for keeping her at school after she had passed the fifth standard, and having her trained as pupil-teacher. But there is an annual new baby in Elly's home; the mother wanted help; Elly must be sacrificed.

Her education completed, therefore, we came upon her henceforth, a coarse brown apron reaching from neck to heels tied about her short, broad figure, her bare arms gleaming as she dashed the water from her brush, scrubbing with noisy energy the red-tiled floor of the living room, washing down the bricks outside the cottage door. We met her, one heavy baby weighing upon her arm, another toddling at her skirts, taking the air in the vicinity of her home.

Ben Pitcher and his eldest boy work on the Brightlands Farm. His cottage stands in a field away from the rest of the village, and looks out upon the Brightlands orchard.

A favourite spot with all the little Pitchers is the orchard, and many a beating did Elly get through her predilection for the place. It held greater attraction for her and her little charges than the speedwells, blue as their eyes, the golden cowslips, the white dead-nettle, about which the bees made such a humming in that favoured locality. The Pitchers' family is fond of apple-dumpling, apple-pie, apple raw, and apple baked; and it is foolishly credulous of Pitcher himself to believe that all the fruit consumed at his table comes off the one not too fertile apple tree in his own back garden.

Yet now and again the owners of the orchard complain. Now and again the neighbours tell tales. Now and again the farm servants, on some blustering autumn day, a linen basket swung between them, their caps awry, their hair blown into their eyes, come laughing and galloping over the meadows to pick up the windfalls in the orchard. Then, sad to say, although the apples are nearly fit to gather, although the gale has lasted all night, they find none. On occasions such as these Elly is always beaten.

He is a tall, silent, dark man, hollow of cheek, sharp-featured, Elly's father, and both she and her mother hold him in greater dread than anything in earth or hell or heaven. Both deceive him and play into each other's hands.

Those constantly recurring babies (there are seven younger than Elly, and there is one boy older than herself) keep the Pitchers' establishment a very poor one. There is a constant effort to make the twelve or thirteen shillings stretch from one pay-day to the next.

With the assistance of our Mary, who knows the ins and outs of many such poor households, I have tried to parcel out the little income to the best advantage. I am told that I must allow to the man, his wife, his five eldest children half a stone of flour each a week. A shilling must always be laid aside for rent; at least sixpence for keeping up the club money. Coal, oil, candles, little groceries must be bought. The head of the family is always a smoker, and he keeps back a shilling a week for tobacco and beer. A piece of meat has to be provided at least once a day for the father and the working son. With what remains shoe-leather and raiment must be supplied for eleven persons.

In the Pitchers' case the eldest boy earns his three shillings and sixpence a week, which goes into the general fund; but he must be better fed and better shod than those who can stay at home, and costs at present as much as he earns. Then there is the extra money at harvest time; but extra food has to be found also, beer must be supplied, if it is nothing more than the watery decoction brewed at home. In the case of a wet, long harvest all profit disappears. Also there are the heavily wet days of winter when no field work can be done. The farmer, poor struggling wretch, is glad to save the day's wage and dismisses his labourers to their homes. A few such days, and there are bound to be several in the year, soon neutralise the poor advantages of the harvest.

"How is it done?" I ask of Mary. "How does this outwardly patient great army of workers, almost silent so far as any utterance of theirs reaches the outer world, struggle on, decently accoutred, apparently fairly nourished, in a measure holding their own?"

"Some on 'em do it by denyin' of theirselves," Mary tells me, "and some on 'em by a gettin' inter debt."

Mary's solution of the problem does not strike me as particularly happy, but for all my efforts I can find none of my own.

Week out, week in, on such tables as that of the Pitcher family no meat appears, with the exception of that apportioned to the two bread-winners; little but bread and cheese and potatoes, and those apples which Elly shakes down from the orchard trees.

It was a nasty implement, that with which Ben Pitcher corrected the failings of his daughter, but it was handy too — the belt he wore to strap his coarse trousers about his waist. It was a belt that was in the army once, like the grey great-coat he put on over his sleeved jacket on Sundays, and it was ornamented with clasps and buckles, which raised ugly lumps on Elly's head and cut her bare arms and shoulders. And Elly was not built in the heroic mould at all; she maddened her father to greater exertions by yelling lustily before her punishment began. The cottage stands in a lonely spot, and there was no one but the mother to hear Elly's cries, to comfort her when she ran in, bruised and beside herself with rage and hate and terror, to fling herself face downward on the bit of carpet before the fire.

Small wonder that mother and child connived at deceiving this husband and father, at once so passionate and so sullen.

In all ways they deceived him. Elly's mother, despite the dragging upon her of the constant babies, is a pretty woman still. She is wonderful to relate, light-hearted too; and although her figure is no more, her skin is almost as pink and white as Elly's. Her hair was once like Elly's too, and for all its careless keeping and rough treatment is of a pretty colour still, and breaks into little roughened waves about her forehead as does Elly's own.

When Elly and she, shutting up two or three of the older children in the cottage and carrying a couple of babies with them, tramped the six miles to Runwich to visit the old father and mother of Mrs. Pitcher living in that town, Elly knew that three times out of four she did not catch a glimpse of the aged grandparents. She sat all day long with her mother and the babies in the long kitchen of the "King's Head." The outing did not cost Elly's mother a ha'penny. There was no stint of old and new friends, frequenters of the place, to treat the bright-faced woman and the fair-faced child. Sometimes they came home with money in their pockets.

Ben Pitcher knew nothing of all this. Elly kept the mother's secrets. Later the mother kept Elly's.

To the Pitchers' cottage there was but one sleeping-room. In this husband, wife, and eight children slept together, the littlest in the big bed with father and mother; three of the next sized with Elly on the rickety iron bedstead pulled across the foot of the larger bed; the boy had for his separate accommodation a shake-down against the wall.

Of this shocking state of things Mrs. Robinson, at the Brightlands Farm, spoke to Sir Thomas, her husband's landlord. Sir Thomas is a bachelor, not deriving sufficient money from his estate — all Dulditch belongs to him — to afford a wife. It is a pity, he being a man made for the love of women and children — honourable, unselfish, manly, gentle. He, rendered miserable by the recital, could not sleep of nights in his own not too luxurious apartment in the London chambers to which "hard times" have banished him. On his estate, impoverished as it is, there must not be such a crying scandal. He resolved to give up his last remaining extravagance, his annual six weeks' fishing in Norway, in order that funds might be supplied for the necessary alterations.

So the order went forth that on Sir Thomas's estate a second and third chamber be added to all those cottages at present having only one.

Then was there excitement in the family of the Pitchers. A constant racket of conversation and exchange of rough compliment passing between the two bricklayers engaged upon the Pitchers' cottage and Elly's mother, who is a match with her tongue for a dozen such. Meanwhile a youth of seventeen — the "slab," as he is called — passed his spare moments in flinging stones and lumps of hard mortar at the daughter of the house when she appeared; in "chivvying" her round corners when she ran away; in calling out to her epithets no softer than his chosen missiles in return for the chaff to which she treated him.

Very attractive was this horseplay to Elly, and it lasted on and on over several weeks — months even — for the boy's masters were no more expeditious nor constant to the work in hand than the rest of their kind. So friendly did the boy and girl become in their rough, uncouth way that when at last the bricklayers' work was done and they were gone for good, and the painters and glaziers set to work in their places, Elly's spirits were gone too. She showed no inclination, as her mother at once did, to enter upon friendly relations with the quieter and more respectable workmen who, for a time, hung about the cottage.

"Eller hev finely got on," the village women say, talking her over; "grown a'most a wumman, th' mawther hev."

She was but sixteen, but she looked older all at once, and carried a quiet and sensible tongue in her head instead of that pert and foolish one with which she used to make herself enemies among her kind.

Presently Elly tired at the wash-tub and fainted among the dirty water as she was scrubbing the floor. Then there came a day when she went on foot with her mother to a town ten miles distant, where the bricklayers, who besides building another chamber to her home had made such an epoch in Elly Pitcher's life, were at work.

It was on the evening of their return, Elly sitting listless and weary in the chimney corner, her head fallen against the wall, that Mrs. Pitcher broached to her husband a scheme for sending the girl to service at last.

"O' course! Ha'n't I allust said it? An' oughter ha' gone suner. She be on'y a duin' yer wark hare. Du yer good to be a duin' on it yerself."

"She be a gettin' a right big gal," the mother acquiesces. "She'll be a duin' harself good and a larnin' harself, as I tell her."

She gives a glance of wistful encouragement at Elly, who, however, begins to cry hopelessly.

"I sholl miss the baby and my little brawthers," she says, and sobs and snivels, so drearily that her father with a warning scowl on his face begins to unbuckle his trouser-strap.

So, in a week or two Elly went away. A place was found for her in that public-house at Runwich with which she was already familiar. She wrote miserable letters home to her "dere father and mother," sending many kisses to the baby and the "little brawthers," and complaining — safe away from the strap with the leather buckle — of the hardships of the place, of the tiredness of her legs, of how her hands are chapped and her feet swell, of how the whole work of the house is put on her, of how she longs to be at home again.

"Send me a flower, O Dere father and mother, ef tis only a Dasy out of the grarse. I fare so to long to look at somthin from dulditch," one of the letters concludes.

The poor little "brawthers" missed their sister sadly, for Elly, by no means neglectful of the salutary rod, yet had all the small hearts in her possession. The baby but one grew up quite bandy-legged through having to be put too early upon his feet. There was no one so quick as Elly at seeing birds' nests, so expert at cowslip balls and daisy chains, so successful with the whistles and pop-guns made from the "hilder" branch. Spring was robbed of half its pleasures for the little Pitchers that year. Mother, too, had grown so "short" with them all, and the children saw her more than once "making a face" and crying quite openly into the wash-tub; and now and again as she knelt upon the hearth, splash would come a great tear upon the potatoes she was peeling for supper.

She has the "neuralisy awful in her hid," she tells the father apologetically, and gets small comfort from that quarter.

One summer evening, when the sweet dusk had fallen and the scent of the lime trees was heavy in the air, when the children had been long abed, and the snores of the master of the house could be heard as far as the little garden gate, against which Mrs. Pitcher, on the look out for a chance gossip with a passing neighbour, leaned, Elly, poor child, came home.

So fagged and weary was she with the walk, so worn out and exhausted, that before she could complete her story

— broken and disjointed, it is true, but in the telling of which not one word, alas! was needed — she had fallen asleep upon the bank on which she had sunk down.

She was put to bed in that second chamber, the building of which had cost her so dear, and the father goes to his work in the morning unawares, for the wife, lying weeping out the hours beside him, dares not tell him that his daughter has come back.

However, in such houses secrets cannot long be kept, and when he returns for his midday meal he is confronted by Elly, her blue eyes wide with terror of him, as she sits on the stool in the chimney corner.

"What air yu back for till yu was guv' lave?" he demands of her, stopping with a suspicious scowl upon the threshold.

"I come becos I had tu, faather," Elly says, with a pitiful twitching of the lips; her voice is thick with fear. She dares not turn away her eyes from him to look at her mother, but stealthily puts out a shaking little red hand and clutches at the skirt of her mother's dress.

"Har missus hev tret 'er shameful," the mother explains in nervous haste, and stands in front of Elly dishing up the dinner.

Plunging wildly with a fork into the saucepan over the fire, she proceeds to fill a large yellow basin waiting on the fender in readiness with the sloppy "light" dumplings — composed of flour, water, and baking powder simply — which are to form the meal.

But with a by no means gentle movement Ben Pitcher thrusts her on one side, and with a lowering light in his eyes confronts his daughter.

"D——— yer! ha' yu been a bad hussy?" he demands fiercely. "Answer me true — or, by God! I'll cut th' life out on yer."

And Elly, shivering, white-lipped, answers:

"Oh, faather — I hev."

At that a wail went up from the little "brawthers" seated round the table—from the bandy-legged youngest but one, who had been given a hot dumpling into his hands to keep him quiet, from the baby in its cradle kicking bare red heels in the air and sucking at its guttapercha tube. For without a word the father began to busy himself with the belt that was around his waist.

At the sight the mother, bold beyond precedent, flung herself upon him.

"Ben — for God's sake — yer'll du murder, man! — for God's sake!" she cried.

She clung to him, trying to imprison the cruel right arm, but despite his daily diet of dumpling and potatoes the man had strength in that hour of his fury and savagely flung her off.

Yet when he reached his victim his arm was mercifully stayed, for the girl, who had not uttered a sound, had fallen sideways against the wall, and was lying there white and senseless, the terrified blue eyes closed.

The father stood and looked at her for a long minute; then, with words on his lips crueller than the cruel belt, turned away and sat down to the table.

When a man is in a constant condition of unsatisfied hunger it will not do — if the heavens fall — to neglect a chance of eating. The dumplings, depend on it, were bitter enough that day in Ben Pitcher's mouth, but eat he must in order to be able to place them again tomorrow for self, wife, and children upon the board.

The mother dared not stop in her duties of the table to show any attention to the unconscious Elly. But before the meal was over the girl had revived and was taken with strong shivering, which she strove vainly to repress by hugging herself tightly in her locked arms and pressing against the wall. Her teeth chattered loudly in her mouth. The "little brawthers" regarded her open-mouthed, and Bandy-legs,

Elly is not afraid of her father now ...

leaning, dumpling in fist, against his sister's knee, gave a burst of delighted laughter, evidently thinking it an entertainment arranged for his benefit.

Ben, having concluded his repast, pulled forward over his brow the hat he always wore at the back of his head in the house, and pushing his chair from the table with a grating noise, got up and went to the door. There he paused for a minute, looking out beneath the blue fields of heaven over the sleepy summer land. Nothing of the peace and the sweetness of the sweet and peaceful spot and hour were in Ben Pitcher's heart. Presently he turned his head back into the cottage-room and looked at the girl. She was shaking still with such violence that the rickety chair on which she sat rocked noisily with her.

"Don't le' me find yu hare, in home o' mine, when I come back ter-night — du I'll kill yer," he said. Said it savagely, but convincingly too, with the tone of a man who quite possibly might keep his word.

Then he went.

So, on that same afternoon, when the heat of the day was at its height, Elly, loudly sobbing, said good-byes to babies and little brawthers, to mother, giving the baby refreshment at the open door, her face made up like the face of a little child for weeping, after the artless manner of the poor, her tears falling on her bare bosom.

Poor Mrs. Pitcher was fagged out with emotion and the day's work; the kitchen had still to be "redd up," and there was the evening meal to see to, and the home-coming of her lord and master to attend. She could not accompany Elly even half a mile of her weary way, but she looked after the girl's short, broad figure yearningly as she went, the mother's eyes all but blinded with the tears she was too much occupied to wipe away.

Across the fields poor Elly journeyed to the workhouse.

The sorrel pats against her weary feet as she goes, the

hem of her pink cotton dress fans away the dandelion-down by the grassy roadway. What a road for such young feet to travel! What a burden of terror and of sorrow for such baby shoulders to bear! For if in the eyes of the law, which permits her father to turn her from his door at the age of sixteen, Elly is a responsible person, morally she is but an infant still. No bird, with its "little life of bush and brier," should have been more joyous of spirit and condition than she.

Elly has lived all her life among people who hold the workhouse to be an earthly hell, who loathe and dread its officers, laws, and institutions as we should loathe and dread the devil, the brimstone, and the unquenchable fire — if we for one instant believed in them. She has, added to the terrors and shames which are familiar to the situation, private shames and terrors of her own. She is, besides, unutterably weary and sick with painful bodily weakness.

Let us leave the child to perform that drear journey alone. Who cares to imagine the terrors of such a miserable pilgrimage?

When, six weeks later, Elly Pitcher retraced her steps along the same road, she carried in her arms her baby of three weeks old. White and pinched and emaciated she looked, her steps uncertain and wavering from weakness, the light, miserable bundle she carried weighing like lead in her arms.

A few yards she dragged along the weary way, and giddy, trembling, sat down to rest; then, rising with painful effort, dragged a few feet more. After hours of such painful resting, such cruel toiling, reached the cottage door once more.

The little "brawthers" were still at school at that hour, the mother was standing at the wash-tub. As Elly's figure darkened the door Mrs. Pitcher looked up, and the women gazed into each other's eyes.

Elly does not utter a sound, but the mother, recoiling for a moment, with a cry rushes forward, pulls the child almost violently from the girl's arms, and turns away sobbing wildly as she rocks the baby on her own breast.

Elly's voice is hollow, all the childish ring of it gone.

"Mother, I cou'n't stop theer. I tried, but I cou'n't," she said. "Yu mus' kape th' baby, mother. I'll wark and pay yer for it. She'll du as yar baby du. She's so wake, she 'ont take much. Kape her out o' faather's waay — don't let 'm strap her — not yit. She's sech a little un — yit."

She had come in and was sat down, and the mother, regarding her with woful eyes, had placed food before her.

"I bain't hungry and I 'ont stop, 'cause o' faather," Elly says, and, staggering, gets to her feet again.

"Wheer be yu a goin' i' that plight, gal?" the mother asks, fretful and helpless, and is told that Elly is bound for her old place at the "King's Head."

"Missus — she's a hard un, but I warked; and she said as how she'd maybe take me on agin when the baby was born. I ha'n't nowheers else to go, and I'm a goin' theer," Elly concludes.

Before she leaves she comes forward and takes the miserable white-looking atom of humanity she has added to an already over-teeming population into her arms, and kisses the little pinched face.

"Mother, ha' yer seen — him?" she asks.

Not so much as a "glint" on him, the mother declares, although she has tramped many a mile in search. As a matter of fact the "slab," scenting trouble ahead, had given up the brick-laying profession for that of arms and had 'listed, and was already on his way to India. No help to be expected from that quarter.

Not a word was said to Ben Pitcher on the subject of the new addition to his family. Perhaps he deemed it wise to take no notice and to treat the little workhouse descendant of his line as if it had not existed. Perhaps, in the fulness of his quiver, he had really lost count of the number of arrows allotted to his share. He said nothing.

The offspring of the immature girl-mother did not thrive. Whereas the lawful inhabitants of the cottage, they who by paternal right claimed their share of bed and board, were round-cheeked, bright and pleasant-looking, the little alien remained ever feeble and flaccid of limb, white and unattractive. It may be that the weight of its young mother's woe and terror was indelibly stamped upon her unborn child; it may be that it felt in its melancholy little spirit the shadow of its birthplace, of its nameless and shameful condition; or it may be (as is more likely) that the requirements of Mrs. Pitcher's own baby restricted the allowances of Mrs. Pitcher's grandchild. Certain it was that the contrast of the two children nourished at one breast was a striking one.

From being ashamed that flesh and blood of hers should be so puny, and diseased, and unlovely, the grandmother grew to feel a positive pride in the child's diminutiveness and feeble condition. The "quality" interested themselves. The "missus," as she was called in the Pitcher family, that is the wife of Mr. Robinson at the Brightlands Farm, having exhausted her own specifics, insisted on driving Mrs. Pitcher and the baby into Runwich to see the doctor there, being privately of opinion that the grandmother — no better than she should be — was starving the child. Her daughters — "the young ladies" — for whom Elly had always found the earliest violets in return for a left-off dress, a ribbon for her hat (they were of Elly's age and older, but in the schoolroom still), knitted little under-shirts and woollen petticoats for Elly's baby because its tiny hands and feet were always cold. Now and then a sympathising person sent a shilling for the benefit of the dwarfed, unwholesome child; a donation which, thanks to the close reasoning of Mrs.

Pitcher, arguing that what was for her own support and nourishment must be to the advantage of Elly's child, was generally laid out at the "White Hart" in draught stout.

If it could but die! the tender-hearted women say, looking upon the miserable little atom of humanity. If it would please God to take it! But it does not please Him. By the loss of beautiful, cherished daughters, chief pride and comfort of idolising hearts, by the death of promising, healthful sons on whom high hopes are built, whose future stretched all golden before them, heads are bowed and homes are desolate. The deformed and sickly workhouse child clings to its small thread of life and pines on.

Presently it is a year old. And while the babe, a few months older, runs, catching at chairs and tables and mother's gown with chubby, clutching fingers; will make his escape from the brick floor, which is his natural playground, to the garden where the marigolds, with whose dew-drenched leaves he loves to play, grow wild beneath the currant bushes; the unhappy alien lies ever on its back upon the top of the chest of drawers where is its bed. Its thin, wearying little voice, night and day, is hardly hushed. Its face is white and moist and pinched; its little in-drawn lips are blue; it lies always with one shrunken foot and leg twisted the wrong way.

It is not claimed for Mrs. Pitcher that she was a faultless person. On the contrary, it is hinted among the neighbours that she has not always been faithful to her husband. It is certain that she tells lies and loves a glass. Yet is she a good-natured and kind-hearted woman; beyond the neglect of ignorance, and the bad usage consequent on a poverty of resource, her grandchild has little to complain of. Even when the weekly payments cease, as presently they do — when Ely goes without a word from the "King's Head" at Runwich, leaving no address — the baby is still kept fairly whole and clean, gets the morsel of bread, which, its supply of milk having ceased, is all that it consumes.

It is an evil day in its wretched history when Elly again appears upon the scene.

She comes, a girl of only seventeen still, but with all trace of youth gone from eye and voice — comes with a brazen face, a hardened glance; with a loose red handkerchief twisted about her neck; with a dusty straw hat, looking as if it had roofed many a villainous head, pulled upon her sunny hair; with a thread of yellow beads about her throat, and a large white apron girt about her waist.

She brings some cheap tins and skewers in her hands, and standing in the open cottage doorway, with a burst of musicless laughter, asks her astonished parent what she will buy. There is a travelling-van hung round with doormats, with saucepans, with common earthenware, upon the open green space before the orchard where Elly used to steal the apples. She steals other things by right of profession now, having joined herself to the rascally-looking, middle-aged proprietor of the above itinerant establishment.

He has taken Elly to supply the place of the last woman who called herself his wife. There are half a dozen small children who play in the dust of the road, unwashed, unkempt, half-dressed. Another, of which Elly is to be the mother, will soon be added to the stock.

Elly is not afraid of her father now, alas! She stands, arms akimbo, on the steps of her caravan and watches him as he goes slouching to his evening meal.

At a word from his wife he comes to the door of the cottage, looks across to the green, and is greeted by a burst of laughter from the girl. With the finger of scorn she points him out to the pock-marked scoundrel with the earrings who is her mate. The owner of herself and the caravan acknowledges this species of introduction by a volley of abusive language addressed to Elly herself and her father impartially.

The girl does not care. That poor woman whose successor she is, died from ill-treatment, and this Elly knows. But he has not begun to beat her yet.

Ben Pitcher is not a man to be laughed at with impunity. A word to his master "up to the house" brings Mr. Robinson, who hates gipsies as Betsy Trotwood hated donkeys, upon the scene. He did not forget in a hurry the volley of oaths with which the pock-marked gentleman of the earrings received his order to depart, nor the string of abusive slang(happily as Dutch to his simple ears) with which Elly, from the vantage-ground of the caravan, greeted that old master to whom, with a nervous recollection of apples misappropriated, she had been used to curtsey.

Before they started — they prepared for departure as the darkness of the summer night came on — Elly's mother came across, weeping, with the grandchild in her arms. Ben had turned it out of doors.

The grandmother kissed the poor waif passionately, with many tears, before she left it; lay and wept all night, her own children sleeping around her, for the poor outcast journeying away from her under the stars.

But what is the small bundle of whining humanity to Elly?

When, in the first blush of morning, the caravan came to anchor again, the owner, having walked at his horses' heads all night, unharnessed the tired beasts, hobbled them for their search for a well-earned breakfast on the short, springy turf of the heath, and went to fling himself, all dressed as he was, upon his bed. To find yet another occupant of his already overcrowded couch was not a pleasant surprise to him. Elly had to explain the new-comer's presence there as best she could.

She was rewarded by her first experience of the weight of that heavy hand which had beat the life out of the other woman.

The greater part of the long summer day Elly spent sitting

at a distance from the caravan, the babe, whose wailing no instinct or experience taught her to hush, in her lap.

All about are little hillocks of wild thyme. She crushes the plant with her elbows as she leans back, and the warm, still air is sweet with its fragrance. There is not a breath to stir the harebells growing in a big patch beyond her feet. The sky above is as blue as they.

So still she sits, the little rabbits, bright-eyed and wary, look out at her from the prickly covert of the furze bushes, only half afraid. A sorry sight they see: a disfigured face with bruised cheek and cut and swollen lip; great eyes that, looking out sullenly from under the battered, wicked hat, keep a watch upon the movements of the ear-ringed man going about the daily business of the caravan without Elly's assistance.

When the shades of evening begin to fall once more, and the baby rabbits, grown bolder, scud across the flowers at her feet, and she sees in the movements about the caravan the well-known signs of an early departure, a deep fear seizes upon Elly. She is half dead with faintness, having tasted no food all day; she is distracted by the incessant moaning of the child upon her lap.

She hates that cause of all her woe. Why does it lie there, miserably wringing from side to side its thin blue lips? What binds her to such hideous companionship? What is the child to her?

She had had untiring patience with those dragging babies of her mother's, beneath whose burden her own growth had been stunted; she had loved and wept for the "little brawthers"; but it seemed as if all that girlish tenderness of heart had left her with its innocency. Nothing but hardness was in her breast to-night — that and a desperate anxiety not to be left behind.

The eldest of the vagrant children, brown of face, white-haired, was sent to bring in the hobbled horses. She watched each led across the uneven ground, its reluctance met by kicks and blows of the small tyrant of seven summers who had it in charge. She laid the baby beneath the little hillock of wild thyme and, breathless, rose to her knees — rose to her feet, trembling with eagerness, sick with fear. Would he go and leave her so?

He had knocked her about cruelly that morning; he had had no thought of the child she was soon to bear to him, but had half killed her in his stupid, brutal rage, but would he leave her so?

The sun had set. The eastern sky was glorious in crimson and gold, the heavens above her head were flushed through their pearly tints by a divine rosiness. The horses' heads were turned to the west. She put her hands above her straining eyes and looked and looked, then called the man's name with hoarse anxiety.

"John, John, I'm hare! Don't lave me, John."

But there was no strength in the weakly voice. In the noise of departure it was drowned. The children tumbled one after the other into the caravan, the man at the leader's head cut the air with his whip; with a strain and a jolt the creaking, cumbrous machine started.

Her hands still shading her eyes, Elly followed, stumbling over the ant-heaps, the hillocks of moss and wild thyme, the prickly gorse catching at the hem of her dress.

An hour later the man, having occasion to stop his horses, becomes aware of the broad, short figure in the white apron and the battered hat trudging behind.

"You here?" he asks, his speech illumined by the interspersal of many oaths. "And where is your —— brat?"

"I ha' left it. Yu said as how I worn't to bring it."

He looked at her, scowling upon her beneath the starlight, and caught her roughly by the arm.

"You ha'n't made a hand on 't, d—n you?" he asks suspiciously.

She is almost sinking from exhaustion, but she looks him straight in the face. "I ha'n't hurt a hair of its head, so help me God," she says. "I di'n't want it. It worn't nawthin' ter me. A woman tuk it. John, I'm a'most starved."

She ends with a sob, and he lets her climb up into the caravan. When she has found herself food and a drink of tea from the pot which is always on the stove, she sinks upon the bed and falls into a heavy, dreamless slumber.

When they find the miserable baby its misery has ceased at last, for it is dead upon its bed of wild thyme, its moaning quiet for ever.

And the next night Elly passes in prison, having been arrested, on the borders of the town to which the caravan was making its way, on a charge of child murder.

DORA O' THE RINGOLETS

I WISH I c'd du my ringolets same as yu kin, mother. When I carl 'em over my fingers they don't hang o' this here fashion down my back, but go all of a womble-like; not half s' pretty."

"Tha's 'cause ye twist 'em wrong way, back'ards round yer fingers," the faint voice from the bed made answer. "Yu ha' got to larn to du 'em, Dora, don't, yer'll miss me cruel when I'm gone."

The dying woman was propped on a couple of pillows of more or less soiled appearance; these were raised to the required height by means of a folded flannel petticoat and dingy woollen frock, worn through all the twelve years of her married life, but now to be worn no more. On the man's coat, spread for extra warmth over the thin counterpane, lay a broken comb and brush. Over her fingers, distorted by hard work, but pale from sickness and languid with coming death, the mother twisted the locks, vigorously waving, richly gilded, and dragged them in shining, curled lengths over the child's shoulders.

Because of the extreme weakness of the hands the process was a laborious one. A heavier pallor was upon the face, a cold moisture upon the sunken brow, when it was accomplished.

"I'll kape on while I kin — I don' know as I shall ha' the strength much longer, Dora."

The child twitched her curls from the fingers that lay heavily upon them and turned on her mother fiercely. "Yu ha' got ter du 'em, then!" she cried. She glared upon the faint head slipped sideways on the pillow. "Yu ha'n't got ter put none o' them parts on, du I'll let ye ter know."

Her eyes were suddenly wide and brilliant with tears; the fading sight of the mother was dazzled by the yellow shine of them and of the richly-coloured hair. "My pretty gal!" she breathed; "my pretty Dora! I ha'n't got no strength, bor."

"I'll let yer ter know!" Dora cried with fury. "I'll hull yer pillars away, and let yer hid go flop, if ye say yer ha'an't got no strength. I'll let yer ter know!"

She stopped, because the sobs which had been stormily rising choked her. She seized in her red little hands the pillow beneath her mother's head. No word of remonstrance was spoken, the faded eyes gazing wearily upon the child held no reproof.

"What d'ye look at me, that mander, for? Why don't ye ketch me a lump o' the hid?" the child cried fiercely; then gave way to the suppressed sobbing. "oh, mother, yu ain't a-dyin'? Yu ain't a-dyin' yit?"

She flung her own head on the soiled pillow; all the crisply waving, long ringlets flew over the mother's sunken chest; one fell across her parched lips. She moistened them with her tongue, and made a feeble motion of kissing. A tear slid slowly down her cheek.

"Not yit, my pretty gal," she whispered. "Mother ain't a-goin' ter lave yer yit."

"Promus! Yer ain't a-tellin' no lies? Yer'll stop along of me till I kin carl my ringolets myself. I ha' got ter have 'em carled, and there ain't no one else to du 'em for me."

The mother promised.

"There's Jim and Jack — they don't want ye, mother. Their hairs is short. They kin play hop-stock i' th' middeer, alonger th' other boys. Both on 'em kin put their own collars on. There's on'y me, what have carls, that'll want yer so. Mother! Mother!"

"Don't I kape on a-tellin' of yer I ain't a-goin'."

There was no time to sob for long on the mother's pillow. Dora was due at school. She wiped her crimsoned cheeks upon the corner of the sheet, stood up and put her sunburnt sailor-hat upon the carefully curled hair. She was neatly dressed in a brown woollen frock nearly covered by a white, lace-trimmed overall; she wore brown stockings and brown shoes. The mother watched her to the door with yearning eyes.

"My pretty gal!" she said.

The neighbour who waited on her in moments spared from her own household labours came in. She held a cup of paste made from cornflour in her hand, and stirred the mixture invitingly.

"It's time yu had suffin' inside of yer, Mis' Green," she said. "Yu ha'n't tasted wittels since that mossel o' bread-an'-butter yu fancied las' night."

She put a spoonful of the food, stirred over a smoky fire, to the parched lips.

"I'd suner, a sight, have a drink o' water," the sick woman said. "There ain't nothin' I fare ter crave 'cept water now."

"There ain't no nouragement in water, Mis' Green. Take this here, instids," the neighbour said firmly.

Two spoonfuls were swallowed with difficulty.

"Come! Tha's as ter should be! That comfort ye, Mis' Green, bor?"

The faint eyes looked solemnly in the healthy, stolid face above her. "There's nothin' don't comfort me, Mis' Barrett."

"An' why's the raisen?" the neighbour reprovingly demanded. "Because yu're a-dyin', Mis' Green, and yu don't give yer mind tu it. I ha' been by other deathbeds — the Lord reward me for it, as 'tis ter be expected He will — and I ha'n't never seed a Christian woman so sot agin goin' as yu are."

The reluctant one shut her eyes wearily; the dropped lids trembled for a minute, then were raised upon the same hard face.

"She don' look like a labourer's gal, Dora don't," she said faintly. "She ha'n't got th' mander o' them sort o' truck."

"What then, Mis' Green?" the neighbour inquired, stern with the consciousness of her own large family of "truck". The supposed superiority of Dora of the ringolets hurt her maternal pride and raised a storm of righteous anger in her breast.

Mrs Green did not explain; the discoloured lids fell again waveringly over the dim eyes, the upper lip was drawn back showing the gums above the teeth.

It was the mere skeleton of a woman who lay there. She had suffered long and intensely; no one could look upon her now and doubt that the hour of discharge was very near. The woman standing above her reasoned that if a word of reproof or advice was to be given there was not much time to lose. Often, from open door to open door (for the pair inhabited a double dwelling), often, across the garden fence, she had called aloud her opinion of her neighbour's goings on; she would seize the opportunity to give it once again.

"And why ain't yer Dora like a labourer's gal, then?" she demanded, shrilly accusing. "Oh, Mis' Green! Don't yu, a-layin' there o' your deathbed, know right well the why and the wherefore? Ha'n't yu borrered right and left, ha'n't you got inter debt high and low, to put a hape o' finery on yer mawther's back? Ha'n't yu moiled yerself, an' yu a dyin' woman, over her hid o' hair? Put her i' my Gladus's clo'es, an' see what yer Dora 'ud look like. Har, wi' her coloured shues, an' all!"

"They was giv' her," the dying woman faintly protested. "Her Uncle Willum sent them brown uns along of her brown hat wi' th' welwet bow."

"Now, ain't yu a-lyin', Mis' Green, as yu lay there o' yer deathbed? Them tales may ha' flung dust i' th' eyes o' yer old man, them i' my hid is too sharp for no sech a story. Di'n't I see th' name o' 'Bunn o' Wotton' on th' bag th' hat come out of? An' don't yer brother Willum live i' London, and ha'n't he got seven of's own to look arter? Ter think as I sh'd come ter pass ter say sich wards, an' yu a-layin' there a-dyin'! Ain't yer ashamed o' yerself, Mis' Green. I'm a-askin' of yer th' question; ain't yer ashamed o' yerself?"

"No, an' ain't." said Mrs Green, feebly whispering.

Beneath the flickering, bruised-looking lids, tears slowly oozed. The neighbour felt for a pocket-handkerchief under the pillow, and wiped them away.

"Fact o' th' matter, Mis' Green," she inflexibly pursued her subject, "yu ha' made a raglar idle o' that gal; yu ha' put a sight o' finery on 'er back, an' stuffed 'er hid wi' notions; an' wha's a-goin' ter become on 'er when you're gone?"

"I was a-wonderin'," the dying woman said, "s'posin' as I was willin' to speer this here parple gownd o' mine, rolled onder my pillar — I was a-wonderin', Mis' Barrett, ef so bein' as yu'd ondertake ter carl my gal's ringolets, now an' agin, for 'er?"

"No," the other said, spiritedly, nobly proof against the magnitude of the bribe. "That'd go agin my conscience, Mis' Green. I'm sorrer ter be a denyin' of yer, but yer mawther's hid o' hair I ha'n't niver approved on; I can't ondertake it, an' so, I say, straight forrerd, at oncet."

The face so "accustomed to refusings" did not change, no flush of resentment relieved its waxen pallor or lightened its fading eyes. "'Tis th' last thing I'm a-askin' of yer," the poor woman said, weakly. "Try as I kin, I can't live much longer. 'Tis on'y nat'ral I should think o' Dora an' th' child'en."

"Yu think a sight too much on 'em, bor! 'Tis time yu give

'em up. Yu lay o' yer deathbed, Mis' Green, an' yu a mis'rable sinner; can't you put up a prayer to ask th' Lord ter have marcy on yer?"

"No," said Mrs Green.

"'No' — an' why not?"

"'Cos I don' keer."

"Don' keer, Mis' Green?"

"No, Mis' Barrett, so's He look arter Dora an' th' child'en, I don't keer what He du ter me."

"Mother!"

No answer, but a quiver of drooping lids.

"Mother!"

At the sharp terror of the voice the lids lifted themselves and fell again.

"Yu ain't a-dyin', mother?"

"'Course I ain't."

"Yer promussed! Yer said yer warn't a-dyin'!"

"An' I ain't."

"Then don't kape a-lookin' o' that mander. Lay hold o' th' comb an' du my ringolets."

The comb was thrust within cold fingers which did not close upon it.

"If so bein' yer don't set ter wark and comb 'em out I'll shake ye. I'll shake ye, mother, du yer hare? Du yer hare, mother? Th' bell's gone, an' how'm I ter go ter school an' my ringolets not carled?"

They were not curled that morning, however, for at the sound of the child's angry, frightened voice Mrs Barrett came running upstairs and seized her and dragged her from the room.

"Yer baggige, yu! Ter spake i' that mander to a dyin' woman!"

"She ain't a-dyin', then," the child screamed as she was thrust from the house. "She ain't a-dyin', an' I want my ringolets carled."

Once, when Dora had announced in the hearing of a pupil-teacher that she was the prettiest girl in the school: "You ain't, then," the older girl had told her. "You are not pretty at all, Dora, but exactly like your brother Jim."

"Jim's ugly! You're a-tazin' of me!" Dora had fiercely cried.

"If you hadn't your curls you'd be Jim over again," the teacher had persisted.

She was a tempestuous little animal. She had flown to her mother with the horrid insinuation, had sobbed and screamed, and kicked the innocent, ugly Jim. If she had not her curls!

But she had them. Even this morning, when for the first time she must appear in school without having them freshly curled, the consciousness of their weight upon her shoulders was a comfort to the child. As well as she could without disarranging the set of it, she smoothed each long curl into order as she walked along. The sun of autumn shone, lying like a benediction upon the land whose fruits were gathered; among the hips and haws in the hedges the birds, their family cares all over, sang lightsomely, with vacant hearts. Happiness was in the air. Perhaps someone would say how pretty the curls were, to-day. Perhaps, as once, blessedly, before had happened, a lady riding slowly along the green wayside might pull up her horse to inquire whose little girl she was, to give her sixpence, to ask how much she would take for her beautiful curls.

Ah, with what joy on that happy morning Dora had galloped home to give the account to her mother! The sixpence had gone to buy the blue ribbon Dora wore among her locks on Sundays; but how the mother had cheered up! She had seemed almost well for half an hour that evening, and Dora had told the tale again and again.

"I was a-walkin' along, like this here, not a thinkin' a mite o' my ringolets, an' I see th' woman on th' horse keep asmilin'. So I made my manners, an' she pulled up 'r horse. 'Whu's little gal be yu?' she say; 'an' where did yu git yer lovely hair?"

Her mother had eaten two bits of bread-and-butter, that evening, and had drunk the tea Dora all alone had made her. How happy it had been! Perhaps it would all happen again.

Morning school over, she was putting on her hat among a struggling mass of children anxious to get into the open, where there was a great blue vault to shout under, and stones to shy, when the schoolmistress from the empty class-room called her back. The woman stood by her silently for a minute, one hand on the child's shoulder, the other moving thoughtfully over the shining fell of hair.

"Don't shout and play with the others to-day, Dora," she said at length. "Wait till they clear off, and then go right home."

"Yes, tacher."

The schoolmistress waited for another minute, smoothing the curls.

"You're only right a little girl, Dora, but you're the only one. You must try to be good, and look after poor little Jack and Jim, and your father — and be a comfort."

"Yes, tacher." Dora took courage beneath the caressing hand: "I like to be a comfit to mother best," she vouchsafed, brightly daring.

"But your mother..." the governess said, then stopped and turned away her head; she could not bring herself to tell the child the news of the mother she had heard that morning, since school began.

So Dora went, sedately for the first few steps, afterwards with a happy rush, the curls dancing on her shoulders.

"Yer mother is a-dyin', she 'ont be 'here long; you must try to be a better gal"; how often of late had that phrase offended her ears! She had met such announcements with a fury of denial, with storms of tears. She had rushed to her mother with wild reproach and complaint. "Why don't ye tell 'm yu ain't a-dyin', stids o' layin' there, that mander. They're allust a-tazin' of me?"

To-day no one had said the hated words; and mother would like to hear how teacher had "kep'' her at her side, and coaxed her hair. "I ha'n't niver seed her du that to Gladus, nor none on 'em," she would say, and would remind her mother how these less fortunate girls had not her "hid o' hair."

So, her steps quickened with joyful anticipation, she came running across the meadow in which was her home.

"Here come Dora," Mrs Barrett, who had been busy in Mrs Green's room, said to the neighbour who had helped her. Both women peeped through the lowered blind. "She'll come poundin' upstairs to her mother. There ain't no kapin' of 'r away; and a nice how-d'ye-do there'll be!"

The elder boy, Jim, whose ugly little face Dora's was said to resemble, was standing against the gate of the neglected garden. He did not shout at her, nor throw a stone at her, in the fashion of his usual greeting, but pulled open the rickety gate as she came up.

"Mother's dead," he whispered, and looked at her with curiosity.

"She ain't, then," Dora said. He drew his head back to avoid the blow she aimed at it, and shut the gate after her.

Jack, an ugly urchin of five, the youngest of the family, was sitting on the doorstep, hammering with the iron-shod heel of his heavy boot a hazel nut he had found on his way home. The nut, instead of cracking, was being driven deep into the moist earth. He did not desist from his employment, or lift his head.

"Father's gone for mother's corffin," he said.

The howl he gave when Dora knocked him off the step

brought Mrs Barrett upon the scene. She pulled the girl off the fallen Jack with a gentler touch than usual.

"You come along upstairs, along o' me," she said.

There was not only the coffin to be ordered in Wotton, but suits of black for himself and children, besides the joint of meat to be cooked for the meal after the funeral. Mr Green did not hurry over his purchases, but went about them with the leisurely attentiveness of one anxious to do the right thing, but unaccustomed to the business of making bargains.

His wages had been "made a hand on," lately; there had been brandy and "sech-like" to buy for the missus; the neighbour to pay, leaving little more than enough for bread for the rest of them. But now, with this burying money—! The new-made widower enjoyed the hitherto undreamed-of experience of knowing that he might put in for a glass at every public-house he passed, and not exhaust it.

He treated himself to a tin of salmon to have with his supper, when he got back to Dulditch. While his wife had been well and about, she had been wont at rare intervals to supply such a "ralish" to the evening meal. Having the means to indulge himself, his thoughts had at once travelled to the luxury.

Yet, arrived at home, he had had too much beer to be very hungry, and the thought of the dead wife, up there, just beyond the ceiling, destroyed what little pleasure the feast might have held.

"Happen she'd been alive, she'd maybe ha' picked a mossel," he said to himself.

That she could be totally indifferent to the delicacy, even although dead and fairly started on her heavenward journeying, was a bewildering fact his dull brain could scarcely grasp. He got up from the table, and taking the unshaded lamp, walked heavily upstairs to look upon this marvel — his wife who was no more.

He was a stolid creature, but was shaken enough to give a sharp growl of fear when, from the other side of the rigid form upon the bed, a head was lifted.

"Hello!" he called. "Hello! What yu a-doin' here? Now then! Come out o' that, yu young warmint; don't, I'll hide ye."

The figure lying by the dead woman slipped to the ground. It wore a brown frock and a crumpled white overall trimmed with lace.

"Hello!" the man said again. He looked stupidly at his little daughter, then pulled aside the sheet which covered his wife.

In the waxen face, with lids still half-open above the dull eyes, with lips drawn back to show the gums, was little change. Beneath the chin a large white bow of coarse muslin had been tied. It was designed to hide the thinness of the throat, but gave, besides, a dreadful air of smartness to the poor corpse. Above the sunken chest the arms were crossed, but, over them, and over the thin hands, in a burning, shining mass of resplendent colour lay — The husband held the lamp nearer, and bent his dull, red face to peer closer at the scattered heap — the miracle of bronze and red, red living gold. "Hello!" he said again, then moved the lamp to let its light shine on his daughter's face, and stared at her.

"Hello!"

"I ha'n't got no one now to carl my ringolets," the child sobbed, her voice rising high in the scale of rebellious misery; "my ringolets ain't no good to me no more. I ha' cut 'em off; mother, she kin have 'em. They ain't no good ter me."

The glare of the lamp held awry was upon the broad red face of the girl with the streaming, yellow eyes, with the unevenly cropped head.

" I thought yu was the boy Jim," her father said.

THE WITCH OF DULDITCH

THE woman who is confidently accused by her neighbours of having formed a compact with the Evil One, and of having until the day of her death exercised her supernatural powers with the devilish malignity natural to her tribe, was far removed in appearance from the popular conception of a witch.

She was a quiet, inoffensive-looking person, with a pale, smooth skin, light, rather prominent eyes, and scant, fair hair, brushed plainly behind her ears, and twisted into a small but protuberant knot at the back of her large head. She was married in her fortieth year; and it was on the occasion of her wedding that she was first openly accredited with the evil reputation which stuck to her through the rest of her life.

For some twenty years before her marriage Queenie Mask lived in our parish in the capacity of housekeeper to Mr George Ganders, called among us "Gentleman George" — the epithet not having been applied to him so much on account of the graces of his person or the refinement of his mind, as for the fact that he is the lucky possessor of property bringing him in twenty pounds a year; such annuity removing far from him the necessity of stooping to earn his daily bread.

Rose Cottage, in which Mr Ganders and his housekeeper lived alone, stands a dozen yards back from the line of cottages bordering the grass-edged road. In the heater-shaped front garden — wide as the cottage itself at the top, narrow as the gate which opens out from it at the base — a couple of large standard roses flourish: a giant of battle, crimson-hued, and the pink-petalled "maiden's blush." Up their stems convolvulus and sweet pea are always carefully trained, and the land around them is sweet with self-sown mignonette. Over the front of the cottage itself a small-flowering, dark red rose grows and blows luxuriantly.

Inside, in the perpetual twilight of the small "keeping-room," there is a constant smell of apples, crossed at certain times of the year by a stronger smell of onions, mingled with faint odours of lavender and dried rose-leaves, and blended with the pungent fragrance of herbs drying on the tea-tray in the window. The window, by the way, is never opened. Long ago, in the days of Gentleman George's comparative youth, it had been fastened with a couple of nails to cure it of rattling when the wind blew, and the nails have not been withdrawn. Strong smells Mr Ganders does not object to, but a "flap" of air is an abomination to him. His garden is as sheltered as a room — his room is as close as a box.

In the drawers of the large press entirely filling one side of the room separate species of apples are kept; the key of each drawer is in Gentleman George's pocket.

In Queenie's day it was as much as her place was worth to touch those keys, to finger the contents of those drawers. She was a woman, honest to the backbone, who would not have robbed her master of the value of a split pea, yet was she guarded from temptation and watched by him as if she had been a seven-times-convicted thief. It was he who weighed out the flour for the daily dumpling; who, with his own "shut-knife," pared and cored the apples, lest there should be undue waste; who counted the potatoes he put into the pot.

It was the interest of his life, this strict guard exercised over his household goods. The pride of his life was that on every day of the three hundred and sixty-five he was enabled to produce from the pocket of his coat (smelling like a cider-press) an apple for himself and one for Queenie.

A tiny orchard was at the back of Rose Cottage; the trees therein had been arranged with a view to apples all the year round, and nobly the intention was fulfilled. No hands but Gentleman George's own were allowed to touch the product of his trees. He kept a suspicious eye on Queenie in the autumn gales, and was always on the spot to catch the windfalls. He gathered the apples himself, stored them himself, was careful to turn each one as it lay in its nest of straw every day with his own fingers. His talk was ever of "Norfolk biffens," of "Rollands," of "Ribstone pippins," of "Pearmains." If two or three of the codlings went rotten, or a "Dr Harvey" had to be thrown away, the fact afforded master and servant after-supper conversation for a month.

But there was no talk in Rose Cottage when once the shades of night came on, for Queenie would not talk in the dark, and Gentleman George did not "hold with" the expense of candle or lamp when there was no work to be done. So by eight o'clock in the autumn evenings, and by seven in the winter, the doors were fastened, the remnant of the fire in the grate carefully damped, and the household retired to rest. Yet did Gentleman George, not a heavy sleeper himself, greatly grudge the hours wasted by his housekeeper in repose. On baking mornings — those momentous weekly events when seven loaves of bread were cooked and an apple-roll made — Queenie was up before the dawn. On the fortnightly occasion when Gentleman George's two shirts and the less important items of the family linen were washed, the poor soul was bending over her tub by four o'clock of the summer morning, the master sitting beside her and keeping a keen eye on the soap. Then there were the brewing days, when a gallon and a half of the liquor facetiously termed among us "guide-ye-right" — because with any amount of it on board you are said to be able to pursue a straight path — was brewed, an occurrence which necessitated a rising in the small hours of the morning. In a word, at those times of the year when the sun rose early enough to save Mr Ganders's candles, Queenie was rarely allowed to press her pillow after daybreak.

But she was a meek and exemplary woman, and never complained. For all those twenty years she had no holiday, as Gentleman George objected to gadding; for nearly all that time she had not set eyes on one of her own relations, as they lived in a neighbouring parish, and Gentleman George was averse to visitors. Such a life had made of the naturally quiet and retiring woman a very silent and timid one. Of the experiences of her past life, of those kin of hers, whom she had not forgotten, although the longing to see them had probably left her, she may have thought as she darned her master's grey woollen stockings, or put yet another patch in his much-mended flannel shirt, sitting on the doorstep, to catch the last light of day, or sitting on the fender, the blaze of the fire on her work. She was a faithful soul, not one easily to forget, and her thoughts of these things may have been long and deep, but she kept them to herself. Gentleman George was not a person inviting confidences from the most effusive; and other companion had she none.

The hospitalities of Rose Cottage never extended beyond the entertaining of a passer-by with a few minutes' gossip at the gate. The only refreshment the master of the establishment ever offered to his kind was an apple pulled from the coat pocket where a few of those delicacies always lurked. He prided himself on his reserve in these matters. He interfered in no one's business, he wanted "no interfarin'" in his, he declared. Friends meant money, he was fond of saying. If you shook a hand, sooner or later it was in your pocket. If every man would keep his door shut, and his mouth shut, and his pocket shut, all the world might be as prosperous and as individually satisfactory as Gentleman George himself. Whereas now "all the world" slouched past to the ale-house, where wages were spent and foolishness talked, or toiled home from labour in the fields to bare cupboards and overcrowded beds. And why? asked the astute bachelor from the safe security of his own position, his rose trees, his apple orchard, his twenty pounds a year at his back — looking out upon the world of fools beyond his gate. Because each man having in an evil moment opened his door to a woman, a crowd of children had come in. A rural philosopher is Mr George Ganders; somewhat blear-eyed in appearance, a fringe of white whisker, thick locks of iron-grey hair, surmounted by a very broken-down black felt hat, framing a florid, sheepish face; attired always in a manner befitting his title to gentility in a suit which once had been black — a suit honourably distinguished among those clay-hued garments worn by the neighbours he could afford to despise.

Queenie had a profound admiration of the wordly-wiseness of her master. She accepted his dicta on all such matters, not even conceiving the possibility of dissenting from them. But she looked rather wistfully at the prematurely aged women from the cottages on either side and over the way who came to their doors in the mornings to watch their children toddling off to school, or shaded their eyes from the rays of the setting sun, looking out for husbands and big sons coming home from work. Often she saved that apple, polished to shininess by her master's red pocket handkerchief, his daily offering to her merit, and bestowed it secretly on a neighbour's child.

Within sight of Rose Cottage, if you stand by the gate and look past the cottages to the left of you, past the ugly red-brick chapel of which our Dissenters are so proud — having at their own expense lately rebuilt it of glaring brick, with large shining windows, with all available crudity of material and architecture — past the small plantation of spruce and larch, where the nightingale is always first heard in Dulditch, is the small thirty-acre farm called Brummles. The name is a corruption, it is supposed, of "Broomhills," most of the land now under cultivation having been, within the memory of the oldest inhabitant, waste land, growing broom and heather. The reclaiming those thirty acres has been a mistake, the present tenant declares, and certainly they yield starvation crops.

"God A'mighty knowed best," this gentleman is heard to say, shaking his head. "Ef He went and planted fuzz bushes 'twer a sign th' sile wor'n't suited to corn. Ef He up and called a fiel' 'Good-for-nothin' fiel',' 'twor a goin' agin Prov'dence to look for good to come out on't."

Here is he, he will continue, "Benjymun Squorl" (only the rector, who prides himself on his nicety of pronunciation — "his finneckin' talk," his parishioners term it — persists in addressing Mr Squorl by his rightful patronymic of Squirrel), "had been fule enough to run agin Prov'dence — which yer might as well bash yer hid agin a brick wall as done it — and hung these hare tree-and-thutty acres o' rubbage about 's neck!" As the "refuge" (refuse) "o' the 'arth," he is wont to say he regards the farm which he rents. "Ay — come to that — th' refugest o' th' refuge!"

Besides his unsatisfactory holding, poor Squorl was troubled with a helpless, good-for-nothing wife. Her one recommendation in sight of the child-ridden neighbours had been that she bore him no children; but perhaps Benjymun, who was of a tender and kindly nature, may have held a different opinion on this point. That she mismanaged his home, made the worst butter in the county, lost all her young chickens, and always had tainted pork in the pickling pot, was common talk. She ended by dying miserably of a cancer in the breast, having given poor Benjymun the miseries of a two years' illness, and left him with a doctor's bill likely to prove a drain upon his resources for the rest of his life.

The duties in attending on her being so disagreeable, and she herself so little of a favourite among them all, the neighbours deserted her in the last stage of her terrible illness, and no nurse could be found. Day and night her husband and herself dressed that ghastly sore, which she all along eagerly displayed with an entire absence of prudery to any stray visitor who could be prevailed on to set foot in her room. Dreadful stories (I have reason, I thank God, to believe exaggerated) of her suffering, said to be "terrufic," touching stories of Benjymun's fidelity and attentiveness were extant. How, in addition to his heavy work on the farm (for poor Squorl had a difficulty in finding the money for wages, and was always "short-handed"), he now had to milk the cow, to make the butter, to clean the kitchen, to do the washing for the poor woman which no one else would undertake, to sit up with her as the end drew on "o' nights."

These tales, repeated over hedges as she was hanging out the linen, called from neighbour to neighbour across her garden-gate as she sat on the doorstep sewing of summer evenings, Queenie heard. Her own mother had died of a "sore" — (it was by that generic title that poor Mary Squorl's dread disease was known among us). She longed to concoct a remedy from the "comfort" (comfrey) root, which grew in the back garden, but Gentleman George at once vetoed the design. He never had countenanced the establishment of friendly relations with his neighbours, he "were not goin' to begin with no comfort rutes" to please Queenie.

But Queenie's interest was kept alive, and once or twice she ran out to the gate and stopped the poor husband, hurrying by to make his small purchases at the shop, to whisper timid inquiry about the sufferer.

Then there came a day when she, having been to the mill for her weekly stone of flour, found that she had a quarter of an hour to spare before her master would expect his tea. Screwing up her courage, she hurried on to Brummles, resolved at length to carry out her great desire to speak a kindly word to the poor unfriended creature who was dying as Queenie's own mother had died.

She had never before set foot in the little farmhouse — in worse repair and with no better accommodation than many of the cottages — but she stood on no ceremony now, for she had small time to spare. Finding the kitchen empty, untidy, desolate, the fire dead in the grate, the remains of the meals of which Benjymun had partaken for days past on the table, she mounted the dark staircase, and, emerging from that steep and tortuous way, found herself at once in the sick-room.

Benjymun was there, sitting on the side of the bed. No fire in the room, although the biting winds of early spring blew up the open stair. But a coldness icier than that of east wind or of frost seemed to smite Queenie in the face as she entered.

"I come to see ef so be as I kin help yer, po'r sufferin' soul!" she said, hurriedly advancing toward the bed.

The woman was lying on her back, her waxen-hued face turned upward; but at the sound of the strange voice — as it seemed, for probably the ears were deaf then to all earthly sound — the skeleton head slowly turned, the hollow eyes fixed themselves with an awful stare upon Queenie's face, and in a minute Benjymun Squorl's wife was dead.

It was a great relief to the widower that in the supreme moment which he had superstitiously dreaded, when the last bodily pang came and the soul of his wife took flight, he was not alone with her. He both thought and talked a great deal of the happy coincidence of Queenie's appearance at the moment of poor Mary's demise.

"She jus' twirled her eyes on her, giv' a gulp — and were gone," he said many times, telling the tale, using always the same phrase, after the manner of his kind. "She di'n't seems no matters worse than she'd ha' done for weeks; but she twirled her eyes on ter Queenie and were off."

Gentleman George of course heard the tale. The woman had been so long a-dying, her sufferings were so great, her death such a relief, that even he could not upbraid Queenie for having made things easy to her.

"She'd ha' been a-lingerin' on Benjy's hands now, may-hap, ef it hadn't been for Queenie a droppin' in," he said, with some natural pride in his retainer, as the neighbours stopped to talk at his gate. "Queenie cou'n't du no less, po'r critter. She jes' twirled her eyes, and —"

Gentleman George, repeating the now popular phrase, would brush one hand over the other to illustrate the perfectly easy manner of Mrs Squorl's departure.

On the day of the funeral both he and Queenie stood at the gate to see the little procession pass, and Gentleman George nodded with friendly condescension to the chief mourner as the coffin was carried by. Yes, Queenie here, his housekeeper, this woman at his side, unostentatious as she seemed, and averse from taking any credit to herself, she had had a hand in that matter!

The poor woman was put into the ground on a Saturday, and the next day an event almost unprecedented in the annals of Rose Cottage occurred. Squorl o' Brummles, on his way home from afternoon church, stopping to speak to Mr Ganders, leaning on his garden gate, found that gate opened to him, and was bidden to enter.

The widower came into the stuffy front room, sacred to all the vegetable odours under heaven, and looked around him, marvelling at the combined luxury and comfort of the apartment. Every inch of the brick floor was covered with carpet; curtains shrouded the window. Sunday afternoon was always converted into a festival at Rose Cottage by the appearance of a red and blue checked cloth upon the round table, in the centre of which a dessert dish, green of hue and shaped like a leaf, was placed filled with apples. Two biffens, destined for the delectation of master and housekeeper, were roasting on small pieces of brown paper on the hob. Queenie, stiff and upright in her Sunday dress, occupied the Windsor chair on one side of the hearth; to Mr Ganders himself evidently belonged the other.

The poor widower, sitting there in his brown velveteen coat, a crape band upon his arm and another on the billycock hat, two sizes too large for him, and coming well down over the long ringlets of his iron-grey hair as rusty as the hat, thought of the uneven, unscrubbed bricks of his own front kitchen, of the broken victuals upon the table, of the cold and lonely hearth. His kind are not generally open to impressions, but he felt the contrast like a revelation. He had heard the word "comfort" without rightly understanding its meaning till now. There had been none in his life. Here, in this breathless little box of a room, was Comfort. And Queenie, sitting prim and upright in her Sunday dress of violet merino, with little stripes of black velvet running round the short skirt and round the tight sleeves from which her red, rough wrists emerged, was its presiding genius.

Benjymun is no more artistic than the rest of us in Dulditch. He does not understand the beauty of proportion, nor delight himself in grace, nor intoxicate his senses in colour. But the way that Queenie Mask's red-braided holland apron sat upon her meagre bust, half covered her full, short skirt, the fashion in which her scant, straight hair was brushed smoothly on either side her high, narrow head and passed behind her wide, white ears, appealed strongly to Benjymun's taste. Looking at her, he pushed the rusty hat a little off his brow as he breathed the warm and heavy air, and uttered a sigh that was partly for his lost wife and partly for Gentleman George's housekeeper.

He did not offer many observations during that visit. The warmth, and the scent of the apples, and the unusual experience of a new idea which had come to him were altogether rather overpowering to Squorl. He felt unusually heavy about the head and a little sick, if the truth must be told.

"Th" p'or soul!" said Queenie, talking him over afterwards with her master; "'tis trouble pas' speech wi' him. Did ye note how he sighed and sighed as ef 's very inside was a-comin' up; and never so much as ope'd 's mouth?"

But if the visitor was not talkative he was in no hurry to depart, and his host, having at length opened his door to his kind, felt a rarely experienced pleasure in showing off his possessions. The various drawers in the oak press were unlocked, and the different kinds of apples lying snugly in their straw exhibited, their several properties of growth, of eating, of keeping discoursed on. The body of the canary, which had hung in the window for a dozen years or more, filling the room with song, and whose death had been the great grief of Gentleman George's life and a real sorrow to Queenie, was shown. Queenie had interred its corse in a moss-filled paper box with a glass lid, having first driven black beads into its head to take the place of eyes. She felt a little bashful pride in having this resourceful dodge pointed out to the widower. A little shelf full of books, which Mr Gander's father had bought for a song at an auction, was inspected.

"They ain't smart 'uns," their present owner said, with a decent veiling of his natural pride in his possessions. "They ain't a sight to look on, but them as know tell to me that theer's a won'erful wally set on this here antikity by the gentry."

He flicked his red handkerchief softly at the volumes suspended by green cord on their little shelf.

"I don't read 'em myself," the master said with the conscious air of one whose life-business allowed no space for trifling — "I don't read 'em, but there they be." He took down a work entitled *The Mariner's Guide: A Treatise on Navigation,* and opened it, showing the charts and hieroglyphics before Benjymun's uncomprehending eyes; shut it again beneath his visitor's nose, and restored the volume to its place between the Rev Samuel Clapham's *Sermons* and the second volume of Bulwer Lytton's *Rienzi*. The other works of which the library was composed were an odd volume of the *Quiver* and a dozen unbound numbers of *All the Year Round*.

Queenie stooped forward to turn the "beefuns" on the hob.

"Tell Mr Squorl about the Cleopatrick; giv' um th' hist'ry, master," she said.

"'Tis another antikity," Mr Ganders said, with an affectation of disparagement. "'Tain't on'y th' gentry that keer for sech."

He fetched from its accustomed nail a small black-framed print which had suffered serious damage from sun and damp before ever it was hung upon the Rose Cottage walls. It was covered with brown and yellow spots, its lines were blurred and faded.

"This here is a French party," Gentleman George explained, his broad finger-tip on the principal figure. "That theer little sarpent she've ketched hold on, she's about to swaller it for a merracle. This here young person aside on her she be a-washuppin o' Cleopatrick. 'Tis a Scripter subjec', and bein' antikity is wallable. 'Twas th' postman, a-callin' to ax me for the faviour of an apple, come ten yare las' Janiwary, as giv' me th' hist'ry."

Altogether, the bereaved Squorl must have spent a pleasant and an improving afternoon. It was his host himself who had to suggest his departure.

"Tis gittin' for our hour for tea," the Gentleman said. "I take my males reg'lar. Queenie, set the kittle bilin", wummun. I'll see Squorl ter th' gate."

"Good arternune, and thenk ye," Benjymun said.

It was to Queenie Mask that the departing visitor addressed his thanks, which might have struck his host—who,

... in the perpetual twilight of the small "Keeping-room" ...

if he had not exactly stayed him with flagons, had at least comforted him with apples, and had shown him, out of his treasure-house, things new and old — as odd and ungracious in Benjymun.

By ten o'clock the next morning the widower was there again, thus showing greater appreciation of his entertainment than the master of Rose Cottage quite approved. He rattled the locked gate at the end of the heater-shaped garden, and Gentleman George, hearing his name called, went out to him there.

"Mr Ganders, bein' onaisy, I ha' come fur yer adwice," he said with great gravity. "Yer a man o' th' warld, wi' book-larnin', and knowin' th' wally o' things, and I'd thenk ye fur yer adwice. My p'or woman's dead; and, bor, I'm lost without her — lost; and tha's th' down fac'. Theer's bakin' day a-comin' on, and th' dairy, to say nothin' o' th' wash —and theer's a sight o' duds i' th' chamber-corner a-waitin' for th' tub — and I'm ter'ble upset i' my mind."

"I heered," said Gentleman George, condescending to bring his mind to bear upon his neighbour's trouble, "the neighbours was a-passin' the word as Meelyer Sprite were a-waitin' on yer."

"Meelyer's charge is high — sixpence a day and her wittles. A man can't stan' agin it."

"A wife's chaper and more ecomical," Ganders said thoughtfully. "Wheer theer's housekeepers theer's all mander of expenses — and theer's waste. Though I ha'n't tied myself up thus fur, I bain't a denyin' a wife's ecomical, Squorl."

Benjymun's face lightened.

"I ha' tarned my thought in that theer d'rection, I don't gainsay," he admitted with eagerness, "and as yu — a man o' th' warld, and allust much thought on i' th' place, and wi' proputty — see northin' agin th' coorse o' my takin' a second wife, I may as well let on as I ha' tarned my eyes on

Queenie. I shall be obligated, Mr Ganders, ef yer'll contrive so' I can marry on her at oncet."

The course of Benjymun's true love did not run smoothly, and his courting was carried on under difficulties; but it came to a speedy and triumphant conclusion for all that.

When once Queenie was aware of the man's intention — and, in spite of the locked gate and the unwinking watch kept upon her, she learnt it somehow very quickly — she contrived to let it be known that she favoured it.

"I ha' allust wished to try my hand at th' dairy wark," was all she said when her master endeavoured by threats, by coaxings, by tears, by bribery to put her off the project.

She said the same thing to Benjymun on the occasion of the only interview between them.

She said the same on her wedding-day, walking soberly homeward in the violet dress, covered for the occasion by a brown ulster of a very cheap and thin description, white-gloved, a black straw hat with white ribbons on her pale smooth hair. At her side walked Mr Squorl, also white-gloved, in his old brown velveteen, still wearing the band of crape on his arm and on the hat which covered the whole of the back of his iron-grey head, and was, indeed, only prevented by a pair of serviceable ears from extinguishing him.

The wedding was not, in appearance, such a festive occasion as the funeral of a few weeks back. Queenie had invited two of her neighbours to support her through the ceremony, but these ladies had declined, giving no reason. As the new-made wife passed her old home on her husband's arm, these former acquaintances of hers laughed with a jeering note, standing in their doorways. A little farther on one of them caught up a white-haired toddler who had run out into the road and hurried indoors with it.

"Why, Meelyer," Queenie said, who was fond of children, "let th' little un be! We shorn't do um no harm!"

But Meelyer pressed the child's head upon her breast and

looked back with a gaze at once frightened and vindictive at the bride.

"Likelies I'll lave my Wulfrid i' th' track o' one that ha' th' evil eye," she muttered as she went.

Gentleman George, leaning upon his little gate, looked after the wedded pair as they passed with an expression of the frankest ill-will.

"Ongrateful wretch!" he said, as his old servant looked up and nodded to him. "Ongrateful, black-hearted wretch!"

Poor Queenie, walking with the strange man at her side, who was her husband, but with whom she had hardly interchanged a dozen words, could not feel very elated at such a reception by her old friends. She had to keep up her courage by the reflection that her ambition "to try her hand at the dairy work" was to be satisfied at last.

And the dairy, under the new management, proved a success. "Queenie werern't niver a mawther to go about things in a halflin' way," her worst enemies admitted. A new complexion was put upon the uneven, broken bricks in the Brummles kitchen. Washing-day ceased to be a terror, whose misery (in the shape of wet linen flapping about Benjymun's ears and encumbering his dinner-table) no longer extended itself over the whole week. The weekly bake became a pleasurable as well as an eventful occasion. His expenses were cut down, but he had never tasted "no sech a wittles" as Queenie now set before him, her husband gratefully declared. Queenie was shocked indeed when she learned from Squorl that her predecessor had "ran him up" at Littleproud's for tinned lobster, tinned salmon, even tinned beef, and such-like "fancical" articles with which certain weak-minded and idle housekeepers are apt to be tempted.

"Theer ain't no support in them theer ertifeecials." Benjymun announced, squaring his elbows over his savoury meal of pig's fry, onions, and potatoes.

Queenie, who, in the atmosphere of her husband's approbation, expanded even to the extent of expressing ideas of her own, had advanced the proposition — become proverbial since in Dulditch — that no woman should hold herself fit for wife or housekeeper who could not "go through a pig." She was now enabled, four times a year, to prove her own efficiency for such post by this process. From the gouged-out eyes, which went into the swill for the animal's successor, to the tip of its curly tail, which formed an ingredient in the pork–cheese Benjy enjoyed so much for supper, there was not an ounce of waste material.

But, although his wife gave satisfaction to the good man who had so quickly made his choice, outside the doors of Brummles dark things were spoken of Queenie.

She had "twirled" her eyes on poor Mary Squorl to some purpose! She had bewitched the poor husband! Why was it that everything began to prosper now at Brummles? Why did the pig fat twice as quick as other people's? How came it that the pork was never "slammacky"? Why did the cow, that had always "gone dry" half the year, now give a plentiful supply of milk nearly up to the time of calving? Why was the butter, that used to be pale and "'intmenty," now of the colour of buttercups? Let Queenie explain these matters if she could.

And by-and-by there happened a more wonderful thing still. Brummles boasted no orchard, but in the garden behind the house were one or two very old apple trees, and growing close to the gable-end of the house was a pear tree that in the memory of man had never grown fruit. Behold these trees, in the first spring after Queenie's marriage, each blossoming like a bride!

This was a memorable circumstance in itself; not much short of a "merracle," indeed, if one omitted to take into consideration the fact that Queenie, in her spare hours, worked like a man in the back garden, digging there and pruning the old roots of the trees, which had spread themselves wide beneath the rarely troubled soil. But a more significant event was to follow. For the first time since the tenancy of Gentleman George the orchard of Rose Cottage was bare of blossoms!

What proof more conclusive of the power of the evil eye was wanted than this?

If it had been that more was needed, look at Gentleman George himself. Gentleman George, who, having tried and discharged three different housekeepers since Queenie's desertion of him, now chose to dispense with those expensive luxuries altogether, and lived alone, preparing his own meals, making his own bed, sweeping his floor, and weeding his garden in tragic solitude, interrupted only by weekly charring visits from Amelia Sprite!

Sad tales Meelyer had to tell of him. How he wept over the food he could not make to his taste; how he was fearful as a child to be left alone when the house was locked at night; how, by the hour at a time, he hung over his gate and looked towards Brummles, only to rush within doors and hide his head if Queenie appeared, dreading above all else that she should turn the evil eye upon him as she had turned it on his orchard.

Was not all this, coupled with the improvement in Queenie's own position, enough to rouse the wrath of the neighbours?

When the autumn came, and Mrs Squorl, mounted on a rickety ladder, gathered the plentiful crop of apples in her own garden, the women drew round the gate and flung stones at her, so that she had to desist. She said nothing of this to Benjymun, possessing in a really fine degree that "*grand héröisme muet des âmes fortes,*" which belongs by right to a certain order of woman; but she left the rest of the apples and the abundant produce of the *Bon Chrétien* (The "Bun crick," Squorl called it) for her husband to gather. He was a quiet, inoffensive man, but Queenie knew very well the women would not stone Benjymun.

Later, Mr Ganders fell sick, and lay lonely and weeping in his bed. Then Queenie put a pork-cheese and a new-baked loaf and a little currant cake in a basket, and ventured within the precincts of her old home. She was not unobserved. A neighbour, wringing her hands free of soap-suds, called loudly on Meelyer Sprite, washing her own doorstep ("lickin' it over," Queenie had said to herself contemptuously as she passed), and the pair, entering the house simultaneously with Queenie, dashed into Gentleman George's bedroom, and slammed the door of that apartment in her face.

Then from the bedroom sounds between a howl and a roar arose, in which Queenie easily recognised her old master's voice becoming articulate now and again in the bellowed forth entreaty, "Kape 'er away from me. Tarn 'er out. T'row 'er into th' roadway. Don't let 'er twirl 'er eyes on me."

Queenie listened, grown pale, then took her small basket on her arm again, and went back to Brummles.

When Benjymun came in to supper, the meal was ready, the hearth clean swept, the kettle singing pleasantly on the fire, and Queenie herself, very pale, with red-brown rims round her white-lashed eyes, sat sewing at a patch she was putting into his sleeve-waistcoat. Benjymun, happily unobservant, made a remark or two as to the bad state of the land, "like a pit" from yesterday's rain, and in five minutes after bolting his last mouthful was asleep in his chair, loud snorts breaking the stillness, the aroma from his working clothes and his heavily steaming boots filling the atmosphere.

Mr Ganders having recovered from his illness, made a pilgrimage to Runwich and had an interview with Mrs Hubby — she who is so successful in the treatment of ringworm, of whooping-cough, of sores. Mrs Hubby is an exceedingly fat and red-faced woman, with an iron-grey moustache and a thick voice. She keeps a tiny shop behind a red curtain, ostensibly getting her living out of ointments and washes, and pills which have a great local celebrity, but carrying on at the same time a secret and lucrative occupation, not even guessed at by the clergyman of her parish and the better-class people of the place. Counselled by the resourceful ladies on either side of him, Gentleman George determined to engage the wise woman of Runwich to baffle the Dulditch witch.

He returned from the interview hopeful of the success of the undertaking, but naturally depressed over the parting with the five shillings which had been necessarily sacrificed to the preliminaries.

As the charm proceeded, Mrs Hubby proved herself a perfect horse-leech's daughter in the matter of asking for more. Again and again had Gentleman George to put that unwilling hand of his into his breeches' pocket in search of crown pieces. When the day, and the hour, and the minute of Queenie's birth had been given, after Mrs Hubby had on several occasions consulted the stars and concluded other occult ceremonies necessary to the end in view, she conveyed to her employer the intelligence that for the complete overthrow of the enemy a piece of gold, accompanied by three of the longest hairs out of Mrs Squorl's head, was necessary. The gold, in the enthusiasm of his pursuit, Mr Ganders might have contributed, but the scheme must fall through from the impossibility of procuring the necessary hairs out of the witch's shining, smooth locks.

"She be a sight too deep for th' wise wummun," the neighbours who were in the secret said to each other. "Tha's a masterpiece, that be, what can hamper old Mrs Hubby."

Queenie's persecutions were doubled; the children, with whom she longed to make friends, ran from her, shrieking if they were small, howling and pelting her with stones when they were of larger growth. "Down to Littleproud's" on Saturday evening, where happier women stood, basket on arm, to "mardle" through the process of "getting up" their parcels of sugar and cheese and candles, she was let severely alone. Did a death occur in the parish, of pig, of cow, of child, the disaster was laid at her door. The hunted look which her eyes had begun to wear grew more perceptible after each such fatality; her own prosperity, although she worked early and late to attain it, became a shame and a terror to her.

When the story of the consultation with the wise woman of Runwich reached her ears she set her face like a flint. Her old master, he whose home had been her home for twenty years, for whom she had spent the best days of her life, whose interests still — so much had she become in that monotonous time a creature of habit — were to her above and beyond the interests even of Benjymun Squorl, he to have meant her that wrong! He should have his way.

With a trembling hand she unfastened the small protuberant knot of her hair and pulled out a lavish amount, considering the scarcity of the supply, of the shining strands. These she folded in a paper, and, scrawling in her untutored hand her name and his upon the envelope, despatched it to Rose Cottage.

Before nightfall the three long hairs and the necessary gold piece were in the hands of Mrs Hubby of Runwich.

That was a night of bitter frost; the first sharp frost of the year. The unusual cold awoke Benjymun at an unduly early hour, and he found that the place beside him on the pillow was empty. He had a great pride in the energy and cleverness of his wife — or not so much in that perhaps as in the perspicacity which had led him to choose a woman of such parts.

"She's arter sum'at," he said to himself now, chuckling

with swelling satisfaction.

She had got up to inspect the cow who was expecting her calf; or she was getting the copper fire alight, that her washing might be out of the way before her neighbours were astir. He sighed with content as he pulled the patchwork "twilt" up to his chin, and turned over again on his pillow. With a mate so filled with zeal, so given over to good works, a husband was entitled to a half-hour's extra snooze in such weather.

However, Benjymun himself was no laggard, and when the light of day was beginning to peep in cold streaks through the kitchen lattice he had descended, tallow candle in hand.

The place was tidied for the day, the floor swept, the fire laid ready for lighting, the kettle filled, the table set for breakfast.

Benjymun, in the time of the late Mrs Squorl, had been used to doing these offices after a fashion for himself. He stooped now and thrust the candle between the bars. When the straw, which was the groundwork of the fire, blazed up, suddenly illuminating the room, he saw what he had not observed before, that the breakfast table, graced with its slab of white bacon, its small section of cheese, its pat of butter, its basket of bread, was set for one person alone.

"She've forgot her and me make two," he said with a slow chuckle. He thought this would be a matter to joke the "wummun" about on future occasions: on summer evenings when he, lounging against the door-post, watched her weeding the onion-bed, digging up the first mess of potatoes, gathering the broad beans for to-morrow's supper; or on Sunday afternoons when, no stress of work being on their minds, light badinage was not out of place.

Having made sure that the crackling, spluttering fire had really "caught," he set the kettle thereon, and blowing out his candle, went forth into the biting coldness, the dark unpleasantness of the morning.

A fringe of icicles was hanging on the brown thatch of the house, on the roofs of the tumbledown farm buildings. Queenie was not in the wash-house; the copper fire was not even lit; she was not in the dairy. It was certain, then, that she must be in the cowshed.

But she was not there. The heifer — to whose purchase-money Queenie had contributed the seven pounds which represented the savings of twenty years in Gentleman George's service — had been milked, and was turned, together with the cow to whose confinement Brummles was anxiously looking forward, into the yard. The animals did not appear to appreciate their release, but stood against the door of the yard with lowered heads, their breath hanging visibly in the air, the grey chill dawn around them, the frost-fringed straw beneath their feet.

When the daylight was a half-hour older, struggling feebly in the chill air against the powers of darkness, Benjymun returned for his breakfast. He expected confidently to find his wife awaiting him. But no sign of her was there, and although he called her loudly, outside and in, there was no answer.

"What in tarnation be th' wummun at?" he said to himself, for the first time uneasy and irritated as well as puzzled. All at once that single cup and saucer on the breakfast-table seemed to convey a message the reverse of jocose. Queenie had never deserted him in this fashion before. There was an element of discomfort in the new departure, if not of anxiety.

He poured the boiling water upon the tea in the earthen pot; and then his eyes, roving uncomfortably around, fell upon the old hat and ulster which, except on Sundays, Queenie always wore abroad, hanging from their accustomed nail upon the door.

Then Queenie was not out of the house after all!

He gazed in slow astonishment at the poor garments, seeing to retain, in their slim outline and the unobstrusiveness of their fashion and colouring, so much of the likeness of their owner. Presently his eyes, slowly travelling downward, fell upon two pairs of boots beneath the press, the only two pairs possessed by his wife, as he well knew.

Tarnation again! She could not have gone out on such a morning in the only other foot-covering she possessed — the old carpet slippers, patched and mended, and only assumed when, the day's work being done, she was at liberty to warm her toes upon the fender.

With a shaking hand Benjymun pushed his cup away from him and started upstairs to the one bed-chamber. The room was as empty as when he had left it. He pulled away the sheet, depending from tapes, which hung before Queenie's "violet" frock and her best ulster; he opened the box containing, wrapped in layers of white paper, the hat she had worn upon her wedding morning. All were in their places. Benjymun turned cold with the mystery of the thing as he looked.

She was gone — and she was gone in her stocking-feet, bareheaded!

As he turned slowly — for a numbness seemed to have fallen upon brain and limb — to descend, his outer door was opened and his name called sharply.

"Hi, Squorl, Squorl!"

A small, white-headed boy who worked at Brummles was standing in the kitchen, the door in his hand; his usually florid face was pale, his round blue eyes were wide and unwinking; there had been the sound of disaster in the shrill, high voice.

"Theer's summut wrong at th' roun' pond, maaster," he cried excitedly; "I come that waay to wark and I hulled a stone to see ef 'twould beer — and — theer's summut wrong and I dussen't go alo-un."

Without a word, but with a trembling in his legs and a

dreadful feeling of constriction across his chest which turned him sick, Benjymun stumbled out of the little gate, so low that a man could pass his legs over it, across the by-road and the field where the rime frost, which

> "Enchants the pool
> And makes the cart-ruts beautiful,"

had whitened the grass.

Across the wide meadow, plain in the otherwise trackless expanse, were the marks of two pairs of feet: one those of little Johnnie Lawrence in his hob-nailed boots, the other lighter, less distinct, such as might have been caused, Benjymun knew it, by a woman walking in her stocking-feet.

The farmer ran in such slow, stiff, stumbling fashion as was alone possible to him, the child keeping a little ahead, but ever looking fearfully back to be sure that he was not alone. The small pioneer went on talking excitedly, but without conveying any meaning to Benjymun, whose sense also appeared to be frozen and who could not catch the words.

But when the pond, with its one pollard willow, its fringe of melancholy brown reeds, rattling in the deadly chill of the breeze which suddenly swept across the meadow, was but a few yards ahead, the boy stopped and, turning his face full upon the man who followed, pointed to what lay beneath the willow behind the loudly shivering reeds.

"Yar wummun's drownded," he cried, shouting the words angrily in his nervous terror; "be yu deaf that you can't hare me, mister? Queenie's drownded. I knowed 'twere har. I see'd th' colour o' har gownd."

The child would not touch her. He put his knuckles in his eyes and began to cry dismally when Squorl called to him for help.

"I sholl drame on 'er," he sobbed. "I wush I ha'n't hulled the stun — that hit her flop i' th' face. She gi'en me tu eggs for my supper las' night. I wush I ha'n't sin her."

The pond was but a few feet deep. Only a very determined suicide could have found death there. She (having accomplished the cold journey in her stocking-feet in order that her boots should not be destroyed) must have broken the ice, laid herself down, and deliberately suffocated herself.

Although with Queenie's death the ban was taken off his orchard, and his trees are pink and white as ever in the spring, weighed down with fruit as rosy and golden as of old in the autumn, Gentleman George has never recovered his old health and spirits. He has no relish for his daily apple. He takes no pleasure in his library of "antikities," nor in the Cleopatrick on the wall, now that Queenie is no longer there to call on him for the scriptural history of that "French party." Meelyer Sprite, who does his washing, rules him with an iron rod in the matter of soap, and refuses to give him an account of the candle-ends. He pities himself extremely.

"Things is all at Harrudge i' th' house," he says to those passers-by who speak a sympathetic word at his gate, "and I myself bain't no matters to spake on since that ongrateful wummun tuk and desarted on me."

Mr Ganders has run down mentally through missing the hand that wound him up to effort. For lack of the accustomed prop he has come neck and heels together in moral and physical collapse; and he "bain't a patch," as we say in Dulditch, on the well-brushed, spruce and intellectual Gentleman George of old.

Johnnie Lawrence makes a circuit of half a mile in coming to his work in the dark winter mornings, or returning in the half-lights of the winter afternoons. For Queenie's spirit haunts that shallow pool beneath the pollard willow; her voice can plainly be heard screeching above the sorrowful rattling of the brown reeds.

"'Tis well she chuse th' shaller water," Queenie's old neighbours say. "The mawther knowed well enough that sech as har 'ud never sink. Har badness 'ud ha' kep' har afloat i' th' deepest ocean-sea."

HIS FIRST DAY AT THE SEA

THREE farmers' wagons, brave with red and blue paint, drawn up beneath the big elms at the schoolhouse gate. In each a couple of huge horses in their best harness, the early morning sun shining on the brass fittings and ornaments, the little crimson tassels shaking on their sturdy necks. The first wagon is filled as full as it can pack with boys and girls, their eager faces glowing beneath Sunday hats and caps, eyes glittering with expectation; dumb for the most part, too excited to speak.

"Lucy Stubbs, you have got Horace in charge, remember."

"Yes, Gov'ness."

"Stanley Arch, take your little sister on your lap. She's being jammed."

"Yes, Gov'ness."

"What have I told you about sitting still and keeping your places till you get to the station? All of your answer together."

A big shout of "All of us is to set still and kape our places, Gov'ness."

"Where are your flags, then? Wave 'em! Off you go!"

Not quite yet; for here is Mrs Shildrick, hot and unkempt and breathless, dragging her lop-mouthed, white-faced offspring by the hand, making wild motions to the wagoner in charge of the horses, and shrieking "Stop!"

"Mrs Shildrick, you know well that none of the children under six are to go to the sea, and that Herbert is only five. You have been told many times that he is not eligible."

"He's a-goin' for all that. The Squire, he's a-payin'. He never said nothin' about no fiveses and no sixes. He's asendin' th' schoolchild'en to th' sea. And my Harbie's a-goin' wi' th' rest."

"Stan' back, missus," says the wagoner, who at a sign from "Gov'ness" has started the horses. Flags wave, children shout, the first wagon moves on, and Mrs Shildrick, more wildly determined than before, attacks the second. In this Governess herself has taken her place.

"Whu are yew to give laws, and say as my po'r little un shan't go?" the angry woman demands. She shakes a threatening hand, becomes abusive even. Governess, apparently no longer aware of her presence, starts on a high note the song in praise of the ocean the children have been learning; and that wagon also rolls away.

The third is only three parts full. The children in it are in charge of a young teacher. The curate, who has run up, hatless, wet and wild of hair, a bath towel round his neck, fresh from his morning swim, and a little behindhand, to see the expedition start, is quite unequal to cope with the situation.

"My Harbie is a-comin' in here," Harbie's mother says; and, making her son into a ball, without more ado pitches him upon the wagon floor. The child, who is bruised in the process but is used to being thrown about, picks himself up and says nothing. It is a peculiarity of Harbie that he never says anything, having had most of his wits knocked out of him in his earliest years, and being as good as dumb.

"You know, Mrs Shildrick, your poor little boy would be a great charge if we sent him. The schoolmistress has already ninety-nine children to look after."

"Then, wha's one more? My Harbie haven't never sot eyes on th' sea. And I've a mind as he should! B'sides, I'm a-goin' myself. I don't want to be beholden to no gov'ness. I'll see arter 'm."

"How do you intend to get to the station, Mrs Shildrick?"

"Run by th' side o' th' wagon, if tha's all."

"You'd better ride with Herbert," the conquered curate says. And Mrs Shildrick, clambering up the wheel, hurls herself down, shaken, battered, but triumphant, with a sounding thump upon its floor as the last wagon moves off.

"Because my Harbie is slow of his tongue and ain't so showy as some of 'em ain't no rayson why he shou'n't set eyes on th' sea," she remarks, for the benefit of any who might listen.

Into the antecedents of Mrs Shildrick it would not be profitable to inquire. Her conversation is never instructive — indeed, the young teacher thinks it advisable to keep the children singing all the way to the station in order that they may not listen to her talk — her tastes are not refined. She, no more than Harbie, has ever "sot eyes" on the sea. That she is not influenced by ardent desire to do so is evidenced by the fact that, following in the wake of the school, as the children make their glad way down to the sea, chucking the long-suffering, ineligible one by the hand, she stops with him at the first place of entertainment she comes to. It is a little yard over which an awning is stretched, and in it are set forth tables where saucers of yellow mussels steeped in vinegar are temptingly displayed. Refreshment more suitable for hot and thirsty excursionists is also to be obtained there.

Nor, at night, when "Gov'ness," making the roll-call of her charges, in readiness to depart, discovers Mrs Shildrick sitting on the station platform, has that good lady made any nearer acquaintance with the ocean.

Poor "Gov'ness," worn out with her labours and responsibilities, has engineered her flock safely through the dangers of the day. Through the first mad rush to the sea — the glistening, glittering blue-and-green-and-gold-and-silver dancing sea — more glorious than anything the children's eyes have yet beheld; and enough of it — enough for all of them! through the perils of cliff-climbing; of seaweed hunting; of paddling, and the dear delight of feeling the caressing waves, hailed with shouts of welcoming laughter, creep over grimy little toes, rise above red ankles, swirl about fat and skinny knees. Through the dangers of over-indulgence in the roast beef and green peas for which they are so enthusiastically prepared. She has had their Sunday trousers and best frocks, of such extreme importance to the poor mother who must save her pennies all the year to buy them, on her mind too. Has had to dissuade Mabel Dodd from her passionate desire to follow the organ-grinder who invites her with such strange words and leers and grimaces to dance to his music; to dog the footsteps of Willy Back, known to be cruel to animals, and always drawn to the spot where the patient goats and donkeys stand in their melancholy ranks.

All these dangers and difficulties overcome, here they all are, red faces freshened by the sea, hair damp with its breezes, treasures of shell and pebble and seaweed grasped in sandy little paws — not so much as a cap or a handkerchief missing! The ninety-and-nine all safe — where is the little lamb outside the flock? Where is Harbie, left in his mother's care?

"Mrs Shildrick, where is Herbert?"

"And tha's the question I was about to ask of yew," Mrs Shildrick retorts. "You're th' person in charge o' this here treat. What ha' you done wi' my Harbie?"

The train is to start in five minutes: small time to argue the question of responsibility. "You must go to the police-station and give notice of the loss of the child, Mrs Shildrick."

"What! and lose my train? Not me! And who's a-goin' to see to my husban', and give 'm his supper, I'd like to know?"

In order that she might not be persuaded to alter her mind, Mrs Shildrick scrambles into a carriage of the waiting train, and takes her seat there. "Them that ha' brought the school-child'en here have got to see all of 'em's brought home again," she declares. "Not but what Harbie'll tarn up.

He's a master one for tarnin' up, Harbie is. There he be!" she excitedly cries, and points to where a flustered-looking group of men and women in black emerge upon the platform, Harbie, in his absurd Sunday suit, his man-of-war cap on his red, lank hair, composed, and silent as usual, dragging behind.

"Harbie!" screams the mother, wildly gesticulating from the train window.

"Harbie!" call the ninety-and-nine, with beckoning hands.

The flustered party in black explain the situation hurriedly to Governess while a porter hustles them into the train, which is about to start.

"We never asked for his company; we never set eyes on 'm before. He been with us all th' day, a-hitchin' hisself on to our party. Drowned? There weren't no fear of his a-gettin' drowned. We han't seen the sea, nor been a-nigh no water. We come to gran'father's fun'ral, and this here little un he hitched hisself on, and come to gran'father's fun'ral too."

In such fashion it was that Mrs Shildrick's Harbie enjoyed his first day at the sea.

WOLF-CHARLIE

IN a tumble-down cottage at one extreme end of the parish of Dulditch Wolf-Charlie lives. It is one of a couple of cottages in such bad condition that they are held past repairing. Year by year Sir Thomas threatens to pull them down, and year by year, merciful man that he is, holds his hand. For years he has received no rent; for years Wolf-Charlie and his old grandmother, who inhabits the other miserable edifice, have received notice to quit at Michaelmas — a notice always disregarded. In the one cottage the ground floor only is found to be habitable; in the other, by reason of the absence of door and window in the downstairs apartment, the grandmother has been compelled to take up her abode in the upper storey. With the broken panes from the window her great-grandchildren dig in the heaps of dust and rubbish where is their playground. The door was long ago broken up and converted into firewood.

The cottages are approached by a lane too narrow to admit of any vehicle wider than a wheelbarrow. It is a lane which leads only to these poor "housen," debouching on a melancholy space of grass and nettles growing above brick-bats, tiles, broken chimney-pots, refuse of all sorts, which space was once on a time the trim garden plots of the houses. Between the broken bricks of the little paved way before the doors a plentiful crop of sickly fungus grows.

More than once there has been illness among the children caused by impromptu feasts off the unwholesome growth. One child, rendered reckless by stress of hunger and indulging in a surfeit, gave the crown and glory to Wolf-

Charlie's history by necessitating an "inkwitch" in Dulditch.

He is called Wolf-Charlie, I suppose, by reason of the famished look in his melancholy eyes, of the way in which the skin of his lips, drawn tightly over his gums, exposes his great yellow teeth; by reason of the leanness of his flanks, the shaggy, unkempt hair about his head and face, the half fierce, half frightened expression. He is what is called in employers' parlance "a three-quarter man," receiving only three-fourths of the wages of the other labourers.

He has the use of his hands and feet; he is not a "down fool" like "Silly Solomon," idiot *par excellence* of the parish, nor a cripple like Dan'l Luck, whose leg the Runwich Hospital authorities deemed it wise to leave dangling from his trunk after his accident, the foot turned the wrong way, so that for the honour of swinging the useless member he has to go on crutches for all his life. Wolf-Charlie is not specially afflicted in any fashion, yet he is in some indefinable way deficient. His fellow-labourers will not "du" a harvest with him, and no farmer dares employ him to feed his cattle or to plough or drill.

Yet such labour as is entrusted to him he does with unfailing industry and a dogged, dull persistence. When the vapours hang white and ghost-like over the low-lying meadows, he stands all the day knee-deep in water "ditching"; and he can always be trusted to "top and tail"the turnips. In the winter, when work on the farm is only to be obtained by the best men, and such hangers-on as Wolf-Charlie are invariably among the first to be paid off, he sits patiently by the wayside breaking the stones of the road; or for a few pence he will trudge the seven miles to Runwich to fetch a sick neighbour's medicine.

His clothes are in rags, showing the poor flesh in many places which custom and comfort have ordained shall be hidden from view; his thin hairy chest is oftener bare than covered; of Sunday clothes he has none. When he sits on the long dank grass of the roadside bank, with his back to the wind and his shoulders pulled to his ears for warmth, and feels in the red and white bundle beside him for the midday meal which is to support him till he can look for his bowl of potatoes at night, he finds nothing but dry bread there. He does not even possess the "shut knife" with which etiquette ordains the agricultural labourer shall carve his *al fresco* feast, but he pulls it to pieces, wolf-like, with claws and teeth, looking out with the fierce, yet melancholy gaze over the grey and shivering meadows as he drearily chews his food.

He is in a word the poorest of the poor — a most wretched and pitiable object.

Yet not so poor but that Wolf-Charlie, too, has had his romance. And here it is.

There was, some years ago, a winter longer and more cruel than any in Wolf-Charlie's experience; when a bitter frost bound the land in bands of iron, "its rigid influence seizing Nature fast"; when the saddened sky looked down on a dead world wrapt in its winding sheet; when for even the valued hands no work could be found; and when the poor "three-quarter man" was in every sense of the words out in the cold.

The Wolf was not a householder in those days, but shared bed and board with a family in exchange for the five shillings a week he paid them. For a couple of weeks not one of the five shillings was forthcoming.

The winter was hard in degree to all classes of the poor; no man dared to soften his heart toward his comrade; no woman ventured to give away bite or sup from the children's scanty meal.

There came a day when Wolf-Charlie, buckling the strap of his trousers tightly round his empty stomach, turned his back upon that poor table at which for long he had taken his place. The mother was doling out to her half-dozen little children the morning meal of bread soaked in hot water, peppered and salted; of this for the first time she ceased to offer the lodger a share. The poor fellow said no word of remonstrance, of appeal, of farewell even, but turned his back upon the place where his home had been and on the familiar faces, and took his way along a certain road. A road which the agricultural labourer and his wife travel (spiritually) in many a moment of depression and in their bad dreams; a road where surely no flower should grow, where the wayside grass and overhanging leafy trees should wither; a road paved with bitterness and hatred and a burning sense of injury and all evil thoughts and despair — the road to the workhouse.

No flowers were there to mock the passer-by on the morning when Wolf-Charlie sought the cold charities of the dreaded place; but the icy air cut his ill-protected body like a knife, the hard-encrusted snow of the road sounded like iron beneath his unwilling feet.

A taciturn man in company, the Wolf is given to talking a great deal to himself. As he trims the "roots" for grinding, lops the overhanging branches of the trees, clears a way for the watercourse in the "dekes," his lips are always seen to move, and a low muttering issues forth. With such melancholy, indistinct murmurings, fit accompaniment to the vague, only half-comprehended bitterness and aching of his heart, Wolf-Charlie went his way and was swallowed up in the portals of the big whitewashed poorhouse. And in that village where hitherto his work was done he was seen no more.

In the springtime, when, as we are told, "A young man's fancy lightly turns to thoughts of love," and turns also, as we know in the case of our present hero, to possible odd jobs, easier to be come at in barley-sowing time and in the lambing season, Wolf-Charlie emerged from his place of retirement — not unaccompanied.

In spite of the warmth, regular food, and better clothing which he enjoyed in the workhouse, want of liberty had told sadly upon him. The strength of his longing and his misery had been too much for the body weakened by other privations, and Wolf-Charlie, who was not a favourite with the master, and whose sullen ways and uncomprehended mutterings made him obnoxious to the other officials, fell seriously ill. In this condition there was allotted him as nurse the woman who now issued with him from captivity.

She was a middle-aged woman, with a red and foolish face, with dust-coloured, dusty hair. She had a wooden leg and six children. She had been an inmate of the workhouse since the birth of her last, which toddled along, dragging on her skirts, a child of four.

So, boldly, Wolf-Charlie reappeared in that world which had not treated him too gently hitherto, bringing with him seven mouths to feed besides that capacious, never-satisfied one of his own. In such patriarchal fashion he made his entry into Dulditch, and, getting employment at the Brightlands Farm, installed himself and his tribe in the cottage above described.

It is probable that the idea of legalising the bond which bound the Wolf to the wooden-legged mother of six emanated from the rector. He found neither of the interested parties loth, and met with no such rebuff on the occasion as that with which Cyprian Crook answered a like appeal.

Crook is the village cobbler, a bad workman and a tipsy one. He does not come to church, and the rectory boots and shoes go to the next village, to be repaired there in the odour of sanctity.

"You don't employ me, why should I employ you?" Crook demanded of the rector,who had urged him to make the lady who resided with him as housekeeper his wife.

On the part of the Wolf and Wooden-leg no difficulties were made; the banns were duly asked, and all went merrily as the proverbial bell, until a report, speedily confirmed, was circulated through the village to the effect that Wooden-leg's husband,the father of the six, was still living, and not only living, but living in the adjoining parish.

Neither intending bride nor bridegroom was at all overcome by the announcement. The woman had known it all along — to the man it apparently made no difference. The idea of marriage having taken hold of their slow imagination, they would not relinquish it. Now that the "crying" had made them celebrities in the place, they determined to accomplish that which they had publicly pledged themselves to perform. They would be married or perish in the attempt. They finally accomplished their purpose at the Runwich Registry Office. Having made all necessary and false declarations, they tramped off in the sunshine of an early summer morning, the six children, who could not with safety be left behind, trailing after them.

The bride, arrayed in her one frock — the old lilac print the matron had given her on her leaving the workhouse — hopped along bravely on her sound leg and that wooden substitute which, through use, had grown too short for her, causing her to walk with much pain and caution. The bridegroom, with his shaggy head sunk upon his breast, walked behind her, silent,his hands thrust in those slits in his trousers where his pockets had once been,gaping holes at his knees. So,with one shilling and twopence in hand to furnish forth the wedding feast, they tramped the seven miles.

So, having accomplished their object and expended their fortune,with the calm of satisfied ambition did they presently tramp home again — to the shelter of the filthy room with the empty cupboard,the bare table, the three broken chairs; to the connubial chamber where the big wooden bedstead filled all the space not occupied by the sacks of straw flung in one corner for the accommodation of the elder children. It swarmed with fleas, that gigantic couch; smelt abominably; its four great posts, undraped,used to

The Bride, arrayed in her one frock...

reach to the ceiling and serve the children for impromptu gymnastic exercises until they were cut down, one at a time, in the first winter and converted into firewood.

On this wretched bed in the fulness of time a baby was born to the Wolf, and then another. Those few shillings which Wooden-leg picked up by gathering acorns for the farmers at sixpence a bushel, by picking stones, by singling beet, were stopped for these events; and at such times the family came dangerously near starvation. No nurse could be found, even if the necessary few shillings could have been scraped together to pay her; the eldest girl, thirteen years of age, was her mother's sole attendant for those few days she could lie beside her miserable baby before, with her hopping, painful gait, she must limp to her labour in the field once more.

As has been said, the Wolf's old grandmother lies bedridden next door. You mount to her room by an open flight of steps arising out of that ruined down-stair room, strewn with plaster falling from walls and ceiling, with the broken bricks kicked up from the floor. The old woman has not been down these steps for years, nor will descend them until she is carried down in her coffin; and because Wooden-leg cannot mount the unprotected, rickety stairway, the eldest girl is told off to wait on "Gran'mawther."

Considering that the child is only thirteen years of age, that she has had the worst possible training, and that there is practically no supervision (for when "Gran'mawther" grumbles from the bed Beatrice thinks it wiser not to hear), the work is done fairly well. A few favoured ones among the uneven boards are scrubbed; the bed-linen — the threadbare blue counterpane, the cobwebby blankets, the yellow sheets — is neatly arranged; the chair and table dusted. When Beatrice is particularly energetic she spits upon the latter and polishes it to a quite cheerful shininess. The little nurse appears on the best of terms of grandmother.

The child receives, by family arrangement, the sum of sixpence weekly for services thus rendered. "Gran'-mawther" is not of a liberal turn of mind and has never been known of her substance to offer her small attendant bite or sup.

But at night when everything is still Beatrice noiselessly mounts the unsteady stairs, gently opens the door of the old woman's room, steals across the rotten boards, and with a deliberate, unwavering little hand robs her grandmother.

The poor old soul has but an allowance of a half-stone of bread, a weekly dole of two shillings and sixpence. Her coffers are not over full, her board is not too luxuriously spread, but to the famished set next door she is a feminine Crœsus, a pampered being enjoying continual festival, diverting to her own selfish indulgence necessaries of life needed by far hungrier people.

The dark, still bright eyes of Gran'mawther open upon Beatrice, watch her as she appropriates the slice of cheese, the tallow candle, the lump of bread, which, with few variations, is the nightly toll she exacts. She watches that little marauder, but she says nothing. There is something uncanny to the imagination in the picture of the dauntless, small depredator at her nightly work, and the old woman, glib enough of tongue in the daylight, lying there, voiceless, to be robbed of her cherished store. It is almost as if that ugly grandchild in her scant and ragged chemise, barefooted, exercised some spell over the aged parent — as if supernatural agencies were at work.

But it is more the spirit of prudence than that of fear which strangles the curses on Gran'mawther's lips. She is entirely at the mercy of this abominable child, this unnatural descendant, who must have the elements of a conscience somewhere about her, as, up to the present, she has stayed her hand and left enough in the cupboard to preserve her relation from starvation.

Suppose that, night by night, the thievish imp made a clean sweep of the provender! Suppose, instead of coming with commendable regularity to "redd up" her granny, she slunk out in the fields to play, and left the poor old soul to die of dirt and neglect?

In submission, it seems, Gran'mawther's chief safety lies. Her only chance of deliverance from such outrage is to give up her wretched bedstead, her round table, her couple of broken-seated chairs; to give up all her pride and her lifelong prejudices, and have herself carried to the workhouse. But Gran'mawther — who prays that she may not live long in loud monotonous petitions, which only cease when Beatrice is in attendance, and which are a sound as familiar to the household next door and as unregarded as the soughing of the wind in the broken chimney — would sooner endure ages of lonely, miserable days, centuries of horror-haunted nights, than face that indignity.

So from year to year the family of which Wolf-Charlie is the head goes on. They are scarcely, one may say, in fortune's power — they never can be poorer than they are; their cupboard is empty even of the skeleton of fear.

Yet often, perhaps, the thought of that other husband whose responsibilities he had taken on his own shoulders may have troubled the Wolf's slow brain. By the irony of fate it happened that this man, who had deserted his wife and children to follow a wandering life, settled for a time in the parish adjoining Dulditch (he had kept clear of the neighbourhood while the parish authorities were interested in his whereabouts). Fortune had smiled upon him and trade had prospered. He had lately started a donkey-cart, and was looked on as a well-to-do person. A buyer of rabbit skins, old bones, rags and papers, a vendor of dried herrings, tapes and cotton.

Often, as Wolf-Charlie sat by the roadside, breaking the stones on the heap before him, this hero would drive past in his pride and arrogance, belabouring his donkey, with not a thought or a look for that other poor bearer of other folks' burdens under the hedge.

The Wolf was not a speculative, nor an inquisitive, nor a ruminative person; his reasoning powers were of the smallest; yet surely in his half-awakened mind, in his twilight consciousness, there must have dwelt thoughts at such times which one would be curious to know.

Once, when the second baby was born — when winter was lying, dark, silent and sullen upon the land, when, tighten the trouser-strap round his shivering body as he might, drag the manure sack he wore as great-coat close as could be about his throat, he must yet suffer dismal pangs of hunger and of cold — these thoughts strove to become articulate.

Stooping over the beet which he was pulling in a field adjoining the road, he heard the well-known sound of the donkey-cart approaching. He stood, arrested in his work, his back bent, the beet he was in the act of pulling in his hand. The wheels of cart or carriage passing along the road never diverted him from his work; even when the traction engine panted slowly by, its fire gleaming redly in the gloom of the thick afternoon, he would not lift his head to look. But the donkey-cart was a different matter.

Presently he raised himself, and with a light of unlimited resolution in his eyes stood erect. The donkey-cart approached, and in the lightness of his heart and triumph of his fortune the owner whistled gaily as he rode along.

Suddenly, swinging the turnip in the air and holding it above his head as a signal, Wolf-Charlie hailed his rival.

"Hi! I say!"

The driver of the donkey-cart paused, looked beyond the hedge, saw the shaggy, ragged figure,the hungry, melancholy eyes, brightened by the unwonted fire of purpose.

"Hi!" the driver called back.

This did not look like a man with money to spare for

bootlaces and such-like vain trifles. He did not have the air of a purchaser of red herrings even. The "hi!" the trader gave was unexpectant, indifferent.

"I ha' got yar wife and child'un," the Wolf shouted aloud to him.

The driver gazed for a moment at his wretched-looking rival, then turning back to his donkey belaboured it with a heavy stroke across its ribs.

"I don't keer whu th' devil ha' got 'em so long as I ha'n't," he called out. And so, master of the situation, drove off.

After that rebuff the Wolf made no further effort to detach from himself the burden he had hung about his neck, neither does he make complaint. With an intelligence not much removed from that of the beasts of the field, he is patient and uncomplaining as they.

And the children in some mysterious way seem to thrive on their half rations of bread, cunningly soaked in hot water to make the allowance appear more, their random dessert off hedge berries, wild apples, and the fungus from the doorstep. They are ragged and they are filthy, it is true, but they are not particularly thin or pitiable-looking; they inherit their mother's complexion of brick red; their hair, which one would not care too closely to inspect, seen from a safe distance is a luxuriant growth. Perhaps out of their potsherds, their bits of window-glass, their "rubbage" heaps, and that most prized and precious plaything, the especial property always of the youngest, a rusty key attached by a filthy string to the half of a pair of scissors, they get as much pleasure as happier-circumstanced children may from a nursery over-crowded with toys.

There is something too melancholy in the history of such sordid lives. One stands aghast for the moment, frightened at the privation which those fashioned like ourselves in outward seeming can bear and live, shrinking from the recital. It is only from such a "perhaps" as that above we can regain ease of mind and conscience and go on our way comfortably indifferent once more. Perhaps the toys suffice; perhaps, never having had enough to eat, Wolf-Charlie does not understand how bad it is to be hungry; perhaps, educated in the school of hardship, Wooden-leg does not feel pain and weakness and privation as gentler nurtured women must; perhaps their lot, if one could see from the inside, as it were, is a happy one after all.

> "Poor and content is rich, and rich enough,"

says Shakespeare.

It is comforting to reflect that if Wolf-Charlie is not thoroughly contented, he at any rate does not complain.

THE COUNTRY DOCTOR

"A DAY to be alive in," Nancie said.

For the Fog-month, the Winter-month, the Snow-month, the Rain-month are over; even the Wind-month is passing away, and Bud-month is almost here.

We see the woods and copses this morning,the village on the low crest of the gently rising ground, the grey church tower, the far-off mill with its white sails — every distant prosect — through the purple haze which painters love to imitate. Upon the tree-tops in the plantation there is a tender shimmer of greenness; illusive, because, drawn closer, you perceive no adequate cause for that verdant promise; the branches are still withered and bare against the blue of the sky. Green is the colour of hope, and that faint glimmering is but the joyful prophecy of good things to come. Near at hand the pussy-willows, all fluffy down, clinging to the branch, are golden in the sunshine; the old clay-pit beyond the hedge is gay with the yellow colt's-foot. Spring is not here — not yet; but one of her bright hours has strayed our way, and the earth smiles at her coming.

"A day to be alive in," Nancie says.

There is a blessing in the air. As we jog slowly along the green-bordered road that leads from our village to our little country town, we feel the south wind soft and fragrant on our faces. So gentle is the breeze, it hardly shakes the dewdrop from the thorn,and sets the lamb-tails on the nut bushes only delicately a-swing. From the hedge to the left of us, a flock of greenfinches starts, with a sudden sharp chirping, upon the wing, wheels upwards in a green and yellow cloud, and, loudly twittering still, settles in the hedge once more. The gorse bordering each side of the road along which we are travelling, sparsely flowering as yet, is alive with linnets. Loud arguments are carried on by the rooks from their busy parliament in the elm-tops; a robin on a gate, eyeing us as we pass with a glance all bright and unabashed, puts up his tiny mouth and loudly sings.

"A day to be alive in," Nancie says.

She says it softly, regretfully, accusingly; for she and I are journeying through the waking life around us, to assist at the ceremony which signalises the triumph of Death.

It is the funeral day of one we have loved; and as we drive along, noting with dim eyes the signs of the dead year's revival, Nancie, who treasures such mementoes of her friends in her heart, talks to me of the patience, the sweetness, the cheerfulness of one who is no more. Above all of the cheerfulness; that blessed habit of the mind which is as a perpetual sunshine shed around. What dark places grew the lighter for this man's smile; what poor sinking hearts, heavy with pain and grief and fear, his unfailing hopefulness lifted. His bright, courageous voice was as good a tonic for a sick man as the drugs he so sparingly administered. What a friend he was to rich and poor; what a safe, incorruptible confidant for secrets whispered in no other ear; how unwearied, how brave, how uncomplaining.

Of these things, as we drive to the good doctor's burial, we talk; and Nancie, who is a nature-lover, — she to whom the plaintive voice of the new-born lamb makes a special appeal; who knows by heart the songs of the birds, and watches the budding leaf; who is a prey to that "divine excitement," the love of flowers, — holds a spite in her heart against these things to-day; because the forces of awakening nature are at work in a world where he will awake no more.

Much of his practice lay in the direction from which we come. Along the road he travelled so often, beneath the burning sun, beneath the wintry stars; through wind and rain, sleet and snow; battling against the elements with that high spirit with which, arrived at his destination, he would battle against the forces of disease and death, pain and the weakness of sinking hearts. At every turn of the winding road it seems to us we meet the familiar figure; impossible to realise that the brave laugh, the hearty voice calling a greeting will be heard no more.

Surely, surely the heartless birds should be mute to-day, Nancie thinks; the sun for a little veil his face!

"All that talent, that energy, that helpfulness destroyed!" she whispers on (it is half to herself she is talking). "That magnificent material waste! Isn't it senseless? Isn't it cruel?"

The question is put with a sob which is almost angry; for Nancie, who is a religious woman, has been startled out of the habit of her mind by the shock of this man's death. He had but died as hundreds of his profession have done before him, from an illness contracted in performance of his duty; but because he was a young man still, and we loved him, it had come home to us.

But we are not the only people jogging along to that meeting in the churchyard. There pass us on our road, or we pass, vehicles of all sorts, but most of them humble, bearing men and women dressed decently in black. As we draw nearer to the town, the roadside is dotted with scattered wayfarers — women, for the greater part, not many of them clothed in black, being of the poorest, but with some sign of mourning about them, and always bearing in their hands bunch of primroses, bunch of snowdrops, culled in cottage gardens or beneath the wayside hedge, to lay upon a good man's grave. And as we reach the outskirts of the town these wayfarers become groups, become a crowd,all journeying in the same direction.

Arriving at the straggling street of the mean-looking little town, Nancie's accusations burst forth afresh: "To have finished here!" she cried. "All those fine qualities which might have enriched the world to have had *this* for their sphere, to have ended — here!"

But the window of every little house we pass in the mean streets is lowered, and every obscure little shop is closed; and in the road before the church and in the churchyard a thick crowd of people has gathered.

"Lord, now lettest Thou Thy servant depart in peace," chants the choir, slow and sweet and solemn; and down the church and through the churchyard (for no interments are made there now, but at the little new cemetery upon the hill) the flower-laden coffin is borne to the hearse at the gate.

"Never no haughtiness about 'm," a man standing beside us, with a bit of crape tied round his shabby sleeved-waistcoat, remarks, for the benefit of the crowd. "Shaked hands wi' me wheriver I met 'm. Blame me! I ha' met 'm as good as t'ree times a week, and he have shaked hands wi' me ivery time."

A little girl half-hidden in the skirts of her mother begins to cry. "She's *done*, because she'd wanted to drop her flowers on 's coffin, and she couldn't come nigh enough," the mother explains. "Time she lay a-bed six weeks wi' them burns on 'er legs, she got wonnerful set on th' doctor. We han't got no garden, and only this one tulip in a pot in th' winder; but nothin' would suit but she must ha't to-day, for him."

"There was no one understood my leg as he done, God bless 'm," an old woman who had hobbled there on a stick declares. " 'ntments niver touched it, washes niver touched it; milk poultices, and a drop o'brandy, took inside, is all I iver found to give me aise, and so I telled 'm. He shaked 's hid when he looked at it. 'Kape on, poor soul,' he say, 'wi'the milk and the brandy — the waker the better,' he say; and he give me the money to buy a bottle, God bless 'm".

A consumptive-looking young fellow, hardby, tells in his hollow voice how his wife and he saved up thirty shillings at Christmas to pay off a bill which had been running for four years, and how the doctor had given them ten shillings back again.

A woman in artless, unrestrained sobbing is crying aloud, talking incoherently, for the easing of her heart, of the dead man's goodness to her little boy who had died.

Friends he had in all classes, but his patients were mostly of a class too poor to pay him adequately for his services. Looking upon those tear-stained faces to-day, we decided that he had been paid.

But at last the wreaths are arranged upon the hearse, are piled upon the carts and carriages following; the sun which Nancie had reproached shone upon the flowers, the gentle breeze blew their sweetness in our faces; and, "sepulchred in such pomp that kings for such a tomb might wish to die," our good doctor passes for the last time upon his way.

As we drive homeward, no more we speak of the cruelty of Fate, of the remorselessness of Death, of the waste of tenderness and manhood and courage. These things are never wasted.

"There never yet was flower fair in vain,
Nor is a true soul ever born for naught."

Of him whom we have lost we say no word; but we watch the white-winged plover wheeling upward from the brown ploughed lands in her sounding flight, we listen to the mounted lark singing his divine message amid the clouds. Presently Nancie must get down to gather some violets she espies amid the long grass of a shaggy bank. Mounting again, she holds the little bunch of fragrance against my face.

"Spring isn't here yet, but spring is coming," she says. "'God's in His heaven; all's right with the world.'"

OLD BILLY KNOCK

OLD Billy Knock stood at the gate of his cottage and watched the cart holding his table and cheers, his bed, his sofy, his frying-pan, saucepan, his two chaney dogs off the chimbleypiece, and his odds and ends of crockery, making its way across the fields which led from his isolated home i' th' low midders, village-ward.

A tall, meagre old man, despite his rheumatism and his seventy-two years, he stood fairly upright still. His hair, clipped close where it grew, iron-grey over lip and chin, was dark and plentiful on his head. In his eyes that followed his receding household goods was something that belied the expression of the lean, grim face; something wistful, regretful, almost ruminative. His hat, worn from the moment he arose from his bed in the morning till he flung it from him to lay his head on his pillow at night, was green with age, battered into shapelessness; his clothes, neither to eye or nose agreeable, were patched out of recognition of the original material; but the scarlet cotton handkerchief he wore loosely tied about his throat, gave him something of a picturesque and gipsy air.

When the cart, sinking behind the gentle slope of grassland two fields distant from where he stood, was lost to sight, the old man turned and made his way back into the empty cottage at his back.

Quite empty; for, among the paraphernalia steadied with ropes upon the inadequate looking cart, Mrs Billy Knock also rode.

He minded, when on the top of just such a cartload, he

walking by the horse's head, she had arrived at th' Low Midder Cottage forty years ago, her first baby in her arms, a wild-looking, maturely-developed, black-eyed girl of twenty. She had been free of her tongue even in those days, and had cursed the loneliness of the spot, its distance from shop and from pub, and him for bringing her there, as she had cursed, this morning, with her parting breath. In the interim that wicked tongue of hers had been busy cursing all the time: employers, husband, children, home, Providence, lustily she had cursed them all. To Billy, who was not exactly squeamish but could swear good tidily himself, come to that, the sound in his ears had the inoffensiveness of familiarity. Missing it, more coldly than its emptiness even, the silence of the deserted house struck upon his heart.

Into each of the five rooms of the house he glanced, to make sure, as he explained to himself, nothing worn't forgot. For long he stood in the kitchen, with broken brick floor, blackened plaster-walls; its smoke-grimed rafters, not many inches from his tall head — the living-room of every-day life. That it had been a small, and mean, and dirty room had never occurred to old Billy, seeing it as Home, and nothing more; the fact of its being such a cramped space became apparent to him for the first time, now that there was nothing to interrupt the view of the few feet from wall to wall.

Six children had been born to him at th' Low Midder Cottage, one, born three months after marriage, had been brought there when they had taken up occupation. Was it possible that nine of them had eaten their meals here, had gathered of evenings round the fire?

If, at any other moment of his life, Billy Knock had been called on to give the dimensions of his living-room, he would have said it was "tidy-sized". (He would have used the same words to describe the spaces of Westminster Abbey; of which edifice, however, he had probably never heard.) Now, with a surprised perception of its limitations, he murmured to himself the comment that it fared small.

Yes, it had held them all. The wild, gipsy-blooded, slatternly wife with the first baby; and gradually Jack, and little Emma, Eduth, and Nelly, and Will; and, last of all, Polly, that hadn't been black-eyed and black-haired like the rest, but had favoured Billy Knock's own mother, with a blue eye and light-coloured heer.

He saw her more vividly than the rest, somehow — Polly. He had clouted his wife on the hid on more than one occasion, he remembered, for having chastised the youngest child with her heavy, coarse hand. He, come to think on it, had never lathered Polly with the belt which buckled his trousers — an educational instrument found convenient in the upbringing of the other six.

Strange to recall that Polly was a married woman now, with children of her own. So he and her mother had heared tell, at any rate; for Polly, having been sent into the Shares to sarvice, had never writ nor took no notice of the family at home, since.

He snuffled as he thought of her now, and drew the back of a veined and dark-skinned hand across his nose.

Her mother still cursed and swore when her name was mentioned. "Ongrateful baggage," "Onnateral beggar," were the mildest epithets applied to Polly's name now. Stories of how Mrs Knock had denied herself, and worked her fingers to the bone to provide the shoes, the gownds, the ap'ons, in which the hussy had been equipped for her start in life, fell glibly from her lips. It was a relief to be able to think of Polly beneath the roof where she had been — although he had never given that name to her, or even been conscious of the fact — his favourite child, without the accompanying torrent of abuse.

The others had all left the parent-nest early in their careers. Polly had been the last to go. Had carried his dinner to him across the fields; had sate by his side beneath the sheltering hedges while he ate it; had stood by the gate, of evenings, to watch for him coming home.

"Gi' me boys!" his wife was always ready to shout; (living so far from humankind, with no fear of passers-by or of listening neighbours, they all shouted, unaware of the fact, when they talked). "A sight o' good our gals ha' done to us, Billy Knock! And look at our boys. Look at Jack and Will, poor beggars, ache of 'em wi' wives and child'un o' their own, yet allust a half-a-pound o' baccy for you, come Christmas, and a shillin' or so to git their mother a drop o' somethin' to warm 'r inside, for me. Talk o' gals — gi' me boys, I say!"

Jack and Will. Yes; they also were in the Shares. They had tired o' th' land, and gone off. Healthy, brown-faced lads, as like their father as peas in a pod, his wife always assured him. But they had gone off, and they, too, had gone for ever. Not in the thorough manner of the onnateral Polly, however; for, now and again, they returned from the mysterious region of the Shares to the old home, bringing, each, a foreign woman with a strange lingo, and several white, wormy-looking children in their train. Two strange, pallid, haggard men, — bent in the back, shrunken in frame, altered in speech, in habit, in thought, out of recognition, — who, they told old Billy Knock, had been his sons.

It was not of these strangers, but of the healthy, shouting little lads who had helped him with the rabbiting in the plantations, and sat in this squalid kitchen over their meal o' nights, he thought now.

For the last ten years he and his wife had lived alone. It had not been an idyllic *solitude à deux*, although the situation of the warrener's cottage had been idyllic. When the devil wanted to tempt Jesus he led Him to a wilderness. The wide expanse of fenland, of water-meadows, with their wild, luxuriant growth, their green and luscious beauty, into which her cottage was sunk, was but a wilderness to the wife of Billy Knock. The only life that of the birds of the air, and the wild rabbits, regardless of Rose the dog and the ferrets in their cage, scudding from shelter to shelter among the coarse tussocks of the grass beyond her garden gate. What to her were "the swing of Pleiades," "the light of dawn, the reddening of the rose"? What to her the fairy foliage of the nut-bushes in the hedges of spring, the finches singing among the fresh green leaves of the beeches, the scent of the sweet briar-bush by the well, and the November sunsets?

Unable to read, untrained to think, having very little to do, a woman might weary very quickly of the loneliness of the low midder paradise — being of a certain temperament might die of it, even. Keturah Knock did worse than that. She took to walking the three miles over fields and through drift-ways to the public-house.

She had always been fond of her glass, and not at all ashamed of the fact; debarred by poverty, the cares of maternity, and the long walk to the White Hart, alone, from indulging.

There had been a day in their lives when Billy, having quarrelled with her in the morning for neglecting to mend his trousers which for weeks had been crying to be patched, had come home at night to find her lying dead-drunk, upon the floor of the kitchen in which he now stood. He remembered how in his savage disgust he had dragged her, on that first occasion, across the garden to the outhouse, and left her lying there. The second, third, fourth time he had so dragged, so left her. Then grown wearied and apathetic, had forborne to take the trouble; had prepared his own supper, gone to his bed; forgetting, in the end, to protest when she, awakened from her stupor, would fling herself beside him.

For five years what a life they had led, hidden away from the sight of man in the warrener's cottage! A life worse than the life of beasts. What cursing, swearing, fighting, even, there had been.

That had all been over and done with for another five years. For that period a bad leg had mercifully kept Keturah to the house, with no means of procuring the poisonous, adulterated drink she craved. As far as the man was concerned, a kind of rough comfort had taken the place of the hell he had known.

Besides her bad leg Mrs Knock had been troubled of late years with a chronic wheezing upon her chist; a disease for which a certain quack medicine is considered in Dulditch a panacea. It costs half a crown a bottle, and in its purchase a large proportion of Billy Knock's earnings from this time went. The remedy had, however, a less stupefying effect than the public-house beer; and as Mrs Knock was of opinion she could not live without it, it was perhaps money well spent. When the pantry had been emptied of its few cracked dishes and plates, dozens of empty bottles labelled "Quelch's Magic Lung Repairer" had been disclosed. Keturah was proud of the display as some women of their pearls.

"Look what this here blamed physic ha' cost me!" she called to the man who was loading the cart, and swore blindingly about the cough with which she was afflicted.

Slowly Bill Knock turned his back on that place of memories and wandered through the tangle of garden. Rags of what had once been clothes put out to dry clung to the gooseberry bushes, too worthless to retrieve; tin boxes that had held pickled salmon of a dangerous brand were scattered among the wall-flowers, the daffodils, the dandelions of the beds. A handleless kitchen shovel lay in old Billy's way as he went down the path. He kicked it listlessly in the act of walking, not with any rancour against it for being there. That heap of rubbish in the corner had been the pig-sty. Never, since Polly, who had tended it, left them, had it sheltered a pig. There was Rose's kennel. The chain, supplemented by a bit of frayed rope, which had held the old dog, trailed from it still.

In those long weeks of Billy's illness in the winter, Keturah had declined to drag her bad leg out, all weathers, to carry the animal's food. The poor brute, straining at her chain, winding in and out of her kennel, had howled and barked, night and day, till her voice failed her, calling upon that rough master of hers, who did not so much as look out to curse her from the door of his dwelling. Instead, had come an emissary from her master's master, who had shot her as she lay, too exhausted even to whine any more, at the door of her kennel, but with her eyes still expectant of him who did not come.

Loud was the snuffle of emotion Billy gave as he looked down at the kennel. He had been a hard master, kicks and short commons had been Rose's daily fare; but he was, it was said of him, a wonnerful man for a dog, for all that. Many predecessors had Rose, until her death he had never been without a dog. He had felt the loss of that companionship among the chief ills which his breakdown and consequent loss of post had brought him.

She had been a nervous, sleek-coated thing, trailing her lithe body in and out between the heavy boots which had kicked; often he had felt her deprecating muzzle pushed into the hand holding the stick that thrashed her. A word of encouragement, and the soft, kind tongue was licking his grim face. Not from malice had he ever chastised her, but from an ignorance perpetuating itself through generations of such slow wits; an article of faith unquestioned, and adhered to with the tenacity of stupidity: that dogs are made to be half-starved, to be sworn at, to have stones thrown at them.

The garden gate which opened to the fenland at the back was off the hinge; the fence was broken down; from the ferret-cage which stood empty, Keturah had wrenched the door, but yesterday, to feed a fire which was slow to burn.

He'd find a sight o' wark, gettin' things in order, the new

chap would, when he come o' Monday. Billy Knock did not pity his successor for that. Through all his troubles he had not found life a weariness while he could keep employed. "S'long as I kin wark I kin put up wi't," he had said. He thought grudgingly of the man who would have to get chaos into order.

But even if his rheumatics would permit, he must now relinquish his club-money or remain idle. If he had so much as stirred a finger to help in the flittin', his seven shilin' a week would ha' been took off.

He moved his lean shoulders stiffly in his dirty, clay-coloured jacket. "How long is this here a-goin' on?" he asked himself. "Whar am I a-goin' to do wi' myself, yinder, ef so be as all day I'm to set 'side the chimbley-corner, and can't wark?"

The position of his new home directly opposite the village inn held not the attraction for him as for Keturah. He was a sober man. Neither did the prospect of neighbours' society appeal to him. He had never held with a sight o' talk; an assembly of people was a Bedlam to him. It was an unknown life to which he was going. He shrank from it as nervously as if it were a new world he was to inhabit, instead of a two-roomed cottage in his own village street.

He had promised his old woman to make his way after the cart, as soon as he had locked up the house and taken the key to his master. But he could not bring himself to shut the door, to turn his back on his life there. He did it once; started to walk across the fields that rose in a gentle green slope from the squat, one-storeyed, thatched house, which from the distance looked like a gigantic fungus growing there; but his feet lagged cruelly as he dragged them along. Presently they stopped; retraced themselves.

"Fare as I was theer still," he said to himself, trying to explain the curious feeling he had that all that was best of him was left in the home of his youth and manhood.

It was not until the day, "apparelled in the celestial light of spring," was passing, and evening, chill with a slight frost, came on, that he finally left the place, and, the doorkey in his pocket, made his way to his new home. He had had no food since morning, but he was not hungry. "Them that can't wark, can't ate," he had said of late at meal-times. He was never hungry now; but he was weak, and as he went his long thin legs shook under him. "My rheumatiz," he said, uneasily moving the shoulders to try to shift from them their dull, incessant pain.

He had been warned that it was not the rheumatiz alone from which he suffered. The doctor, standing out of earshot of the patient, had made a communcation to the wife in an undertone. And Keturah had shouted from kitchen to bedroom, doctor being gone, the intelligence that Billy Knock's last day's wark was done, that his heart was 'fected, and might at any moment stop beating.

"Theer ain't no doubt 'tis 'fected. I could ha' telled him that," Billy had answered contemptuously.

Once or twice as he walked the weary miles tonight, he thought that the moment had come; that the heart was going to stop.

As he went through the last field where the young barley was pricking, single-leaved, through the dusty soil, he encountered his master, who hailed him as the old man would have passed sullenly on without giving him the sign o' th' day.

"Cleared out?" the master called to him cheerily; and Billy, without turning his face in the other's direction, admitted that he had done so.

"You've lived in the Low Meadow Cottage a long time, Billy?"

"Forty yare, come Lady-day," Billy grimly said.

"A lot of years, Billy!"

"Several."

"Thirty years before I came to Dulditch!"

"Ah!" The grimly closed lips, the eyes gazing into a retrospect in which the master had no part, held the old man's bitter unspoken reflection, "Better folk than you was above ground then!"

"Have you got the key, Billy?"

"I ha' got it."

The master held out his hand which Billy ignored. "You shall ha' the key, come Monday," he said. The fingers in his jacket pocket tightened stiffly upon it; he could not bring himself to part with the key.

He moved on; the master, a young spruce-looking man, who liked the old fellow, in spite of his uncouthness and his surly ways, walked a step by his side.

"How's your health now, Billy?"

"No matters, the wind ha' been a-shiftin'; my rheumatiz is all of a whizzle ter-night."

"You ought to be at home by the fire."

"I'm a-goin' theer." He looked ahead of him with his regretful eyes. "Ef so be as you kin call it 'home'," he added.

"You're still on your club?"

"Ah, I'm on it. Wheer'd I ha' been ef I worn't on it? Parashin' o' want, mayhap. Who's to keer?"

"If you'd had a decent wife, remember, you might have put by a tidy bit of money by now."

"My missus is as good as other folks's missuses, I take it," the old man said, and turned an angry shoulder upon the other man. "I don't lay no blame agin my old woman."

When he reached the cottage opposite the public-house, he found that Mrs Knock had availed herself of the propinquity of that hostelry, and repaid herself liberally for her enforced abstinence of years. The furniture had been put down, helter-skelter, in the rooms and the little oblong of garden; she herself lay among it, drunk on the dirty floor.

A neighbour, who had been on the look-out for old Billy's

coming, found him gazing down with an expressionless face upon the ugly, unwieldy body.

"Me and my neighbour didn't take it on ourselves to touch your goods while things was like this here," she explained, delicately alluding to Mrs Knock's unconscious condition. "But now you're here to give us the ward to lend a hand, me and her will put up a bed for ye in no time, Billy."

The old man declined her offer without a word of thanks, and turned away. "I don't want no bed, I'll be a-gittin' back," he said.

"Come in, Billy, and get a bit o' supper alonger me and my old man," another pitying woman said.

He did not stop in his hurried retreat to consider the invitation. "I'll be a-gittin' back," he said again.

The neighbours stood to look after him as he went; the tall, only slightly-stooping figure in the shabby hat, the patched, clay-coloured clothes; the ends of the scarlet handkerchief loosely flying.

"He's in a fine hurry to be gone, and no wonder! Poor old beggar!" they said.

For his footsteps did not lag now; he forgot the wearying ache of arm and shoulder; the load seemed lightened upon the labouring heart. "I cou'n't ha' stayed theer, nohow," he kept saying to himself as he hurried along. "I'll make th' best o' my way back agin."

His weakness, aggravated by the day's fast, increased upon him as he went hastily, stumbling on his way.

"I cou'n't ha' ralished no wittles theer," he told himself, shaking his head.

Among the worrying noises surging in his head as he hastened on, the pitying neighbour seemed still to be offering him food. "I'd rayther wait till I git home, bor," he answered the voice of fancy. "I shall ralish it more ef I hold out till I git theer."

"'Fected'! he was saying aloud presently. "I should think

'tis ''fected'! I could ha' telled him that. Ef he was to know how tha's a hammerin' i' my inside, he wou'n't want to be no doctor to know 'twas 'fected."

"I can't bide, I tell ye," he made irritable answer to another imagined voice. Following in his footsteps the people were; crowds of them; the whole population from that strange country by the inn where they had wanted him to make his home; they were hurrying after him, asking him to eat, plaguing him to stay. Through the hammering in his chest and the throbbing turmoil in his head, he made out their words with difficulty. He was hampered to keep up the necessary pace, but he urged himself with difficulty on, feeling he must escape them.

"The missus, she'll be a-waitin' supper; and Polly, maybe, 'll be a-hangin' on the gate."

Perhaps in the end he saw her there, the only little one amongst them who had had the blue eyes of his mother. Perhaps, his journey being done, in spirit he took her hand again, and went once more into the cottage, sunk fungus-like among the verdure, that had been home to him for forty years.

For when Keturah, going the next morning, spite of her bad head and bad leg, to see what had become of that silly old beggar, her husband, and to swear at him for leading her such a dance, found him lying dead in the middle of the last meadow he had had to cross, his face was turned towards the cottage, and there was a smile upon his lips.

LITTLE BROTHER

I MET the parish nurse hurrying from the cottage in which a baby had, that morning, been born, towards a cottage at the other end of the village where a baby was due to be born, that night.

"All well over!" she said. "Mrs Hodd going on nicely as can be expected."

"She ought to be used to it by now, Nurse! The thirteenth!"

"Well, this one is dead. Born dead."

"What a mercy!"

But our nurse does not like a case where the baby is born dead. "Such a beautiful child too!"

"It's more than can be said of the other twelve."

"How can you tell?" Nurse said. "Look at their clothes; look at their hair, standing on end; look at the scenes they live in!"

"The Hodds ought to be sent to prison for having thirteen children."

"Go and tell Hodd himself so. You'll find him, if you go through the farm-yard. In the turnip-house. He slept there, last night; did not come home at all. He always clears out on these occasions. 'A good riddance,' Mrs Hodd says."

Mr Hodd answered my greeting by a side-ways chuck of his head, and went on turning the handle of the cutting-machine which a small boy, working with him, replenished with whole turnips. The father of thirteen was a wild, unkempt-looking creature, habited in an outer garment composed of a dirty sack, through the hole cut in the bottom of which his head projected; a tangle of matted red hair met a tangle of matted red beard; a small portion of white cheek beneath the angry-looking blue eyes was the only part of his face uncovered. His arms, thrust through the slits cut in the sides of the sack, were hung about with rags which might once have been sleeves of a grey flannel shirt. Not such a family as the Hodds do we often see in Dulditch, but in the present shortage of labour the farmers are glad to welcome what help they can get.

"So I hear your wife's given birth to a dead baby, Hodd."

Swish — swish — swish went the knife through the turnips, the neat sections dropping into the basket beneath. Two revolutions of the handle, then a curt, "So they tell me."

"Haven't you been home to see your wife?"

"No." Swish — swish. "Nor ain't a-goin'."

"I think you ought to go. Mrs Hodd will be wanting to see you."

Two vicious turns of the handle of the machine which the boy feeds assiduously. Hodd is 'putting his back into it,' this morning!

"She's borne you many children, Hodd."

"A sight too many!" Swish — swish "The place is chuck full of 'em. You stamp on 'em as you walk."

"They keep you poor, I'm afraid!"

"Ah!" Swish — swish — swish.

"At any rate this poor little one won't have to be fed; you're no worse off than before it came."

"There'll soon be another," Hodd grunted, savagely prophetic. "There's no stoppin' my missus, once she' sot a-goin'."

The reflection that it was hardly fair to put it all on to Mrs Hodd, this way, I kept to myself.

The little boy, pitching the turnips into the voracious maw of the machine, looked at me brightly. He also was red-headed, he also was attired for the most part in a sack. He was the eldest hope of the Hodd family, helping his father in the hour between morning and afternoon school.

"Him and me —," a nod in the direction of his parent, "have got to make a box tonight, when we laves off wark, he said. "Mother, she've sent ward by Nurse we've got to make a box to put little brother in."

"Ah, poor little one!"

"Then him and me," a chuck of his chin at the parent Hodd "is a-goin' to carry 'm to the corner of the chech-yard where there ain't no blessin',"

"Now then! Git on wi' them turmits, boy." In his pleasurable anticipation of the jaunt before him, the boy had stopped in his work. But he at once re-addressed himself to the task of throwing the turnips into the ever-open mouth of the cutter, where they bobbed about merrily for a moment or two before settling into position for the knives to slice.

"Well, good morning, Hodd," I said. "I shall go to see your wife and the poor baby before it is put in the box."

Swish. Swish. Swish.

In the kitchen I passed through on my way upstairs, a pair of Hodds, of too tender an age to be at school, were seated on a sack — again a sack! — spread before the fire, and were playing with a large battered doll. Mrs Hodd, above, lay in her big squalid bed, alone.

"Have you no one to wait on you?"

"Blesh you, yes! There's the gal Maude." Maude was the twelve years old daughter. "Nonly she've gone on a narrand now, to let the parson's folk know as I'm brought to bed, and to ask for a drop o' soup, and a packet o' gro'ts, and a few nouraging matters o' that sort. For I've got to have life kep' in me somehow, I s'pose. And if parson's folk don't do it I don't know who should."

"So the poor baby is dead, this time, Mrs Hodd!"

Mrs Hodd wrung her nose round to the middle of her cheek with a loud snuffle, tears streamed from her blue eyes. (All the Hodd family have red hair and blue eyes; so adorned themselves, and having started on a family thus endowed, Mr and Mrs Hodd had never paused to alter the pattern.)

"That fare hard," she gurgled, "to go t'rough it all, and then to lose 'em."

"But you have so many, Mrs Hodd. This little one could well be spared. Hodd thinks as I do."

"Ah! Hodd, he han't a mother's heart!"

"I am sure it is all you can do to feed and clothe the twelve."

"Clothe? I don't clothe 'em. I look after their insides. No one can't say as my child'en look starved. If parson's folk want to see 'em clothed they must do it theirselves. My job's their insides, I take it."

"I should like to see the poor baby, Mrs Hodd. I hear it was a very fine child."

"Mine allers is!" Mrs Hodd testified. "A crop o' heer he'd got all over his poll like golden suverins. My little uns, they're all that plased wi' their little brother! A fine hollerin' there'll be when he's took off to the buryin'."

"Where is he? Look, I've brought a few flowers to lay upon his tiny coffin."

Mrs Hodd, without lifting her tousled head, cast a glance of enquiry round the almost bare room. Near the door a rude bed had been made by spreading a towel over a frowsy pillow laid on two chairs.

"Ain't he theer?" the woman asked, her eyes upon the chairs.

"Nothing's there, Mrs Hodd."

"Randolph!" Mrs Hodd screamed with starling abruptness. "'Vangeline! Come you here, this minute; don't I'll warm yer jackets for ye when I git yer."

"Pray do not excite yourself," I cried, alarmed. "If you want the children who are in the kitchen I will fetch them for you."

The tiny children on the filthy hearth were too much engrossed with their play to be aware of me, standing to watch. They were striving to draw over the rigid legs of the doll the grey calico nightgown of which they were stripping it when I saw them last. Their fat dirty little hands trembled with their eagerness to accomplish this feat. The mite who had the toy on her knees rocked herself maternally, and gave chirrups of encouragement as she worked.

"Theer! put ickle arms in! Put in ickle arms!"

Failing in every effort to insert the arms, she decided to dispense with that formality; pulling the awful nightgown over the shoulders she knotted it at the back of a little red head.

Then she turned the battered doll on its back and I saw that it was the dead baby.

Evangeline and Randolph pushed their grubby fingers into the open mouth, and tried to force them into the sunken eyes, in order to raise the lids.

"Wake up! Wake up, ickle brudder!" they said.

When I had rescued the desecrated body, and borne it to its poor bier in the mother's room, I spoke a word to Mrs Hodd which she resented.

"Time is long for sech little uns, when t'others 're at school and I'm laid by," she said. "Other folkes' child'en have a toy, now and then, to kape 'em out o' mischief. My little uns han't. He've kep' 'em quite (quiet) for hours, the po'r baby have; and I'll lay a crown they han't done no harm to their little brother."

"Him and me — " "have got to make a box tonight" . . .

THE GAL LA'RENCES

YEARS ago, when our little Margaret was with us still, she startled my absent thought to attention one day by the remark that she considered Hannah and Rhoda Lawrence the happiest women she had ever known.

"The very happiest in the world," the child repeated, smelling at the bouquet of auriculas, wallflowers, and lemon-thyme she had gathered from the little strips of flower-garden which border the tiny path before the "gal La'rences'" door. In reply to my surprised inquiry, she explained that their supreme bliss, to her thinking, lay in the fact that each of them had the happiness to possess a child of her own and neither had the affliction of a husband.

The circumstance which seemed so felicitous to Margaret was not, it need scarcely be said, of a nature to make life unduly smooth and easy for the two principally concerned. Each, at intervals of several years, had gone from service to the workhouse; each had brought from thence her babe to her parents' home, and had gone out to service again — to a lower, less reputable service, where mistresses were not particular about the antecedents of their servants so long as each could do the work of three women of fairer record.

On the death of their parents, dying of a fever in one week, the sisters, girls of twenty and twenty-two, came home, service being no longer possible to them, as their children must be looked after. To bury the father and mother, to pay

Billers new petticoats pinned to those of his nurse

the doctor's bill, every penny of that collection of silver and pence — the paternal savings of many years confided to the earthenware tea-pot on the mantelpiece — had to go, besides what could be dispensed with of the scanty furniture the cottage contained.

The little girl, Becky, by this time five years of age, was sent all day to school, and to set the sisters free for the only labour obtainable, the year-old boy was, at the cost of a shilling a week, put out to daily nursing. Little "Becker," despatched with her slice of bread and dripping, bread and treacle, dry bread, according to the state of the exchequer, her little bottle of cold tea for her midday meal, was no worse off than the rest of her school-fellows. But it is to be feared that the infantile "Biller," relinquished to the tender mercies of Happy (christened Hephzibah) Hunter, must have gone through some trying vicissitudes. After he had fallen among the hot cinders beneath the grate for the third time, Rhoda insisted on having his petticoats pinned to those of his nurse, so that if Happy did fall asleep as soon as she sat down with her charge over the fire the danger to Biller might be minimised. With her own hands the mother erected a guard across the "t'reshol'" of the Hunter door to restrain the wanderings of the venturesome Biller, who, while Happy went about her domestic affairs, had twice been rescued from beneath the feet of horses passing on the road. Biller's soft and hairless head was always swelled in some new direction through being brought into contact with hard and immovable objects; his arms were ever vari-coloured from bruises, his legs were covered with scratches. Yet Happy, who was deaf and blind and without a roof to her mouth, was glad to earn the shilling a week, and Rhoda could find no one else willing to tend the child.

Their children being all day long off their hands, the "gal La'rences," as they are still called in spite of their sixty years and more, went to work upon the land. Week after week, year out, year in, from sunrise to sunset during the winter months, from six to six through the golden summer days, those two trudged off when work was to be had. Insufficiently clad, half fed, they set themselves to labour for which no woman's frame is fitted in order that the boy and girl, poor nameless little mortals with their heritage of shame, should be kept alive; in order that the rent of the wretched house in which their father and mother had lived for thirty years should be paid; in order that they who had covered themselves with a disgrace which, according to our charitable code, there is no washing away, should not stoop to that worse disgrace from the "gal La'rences'" point of view — the disgrace of asking for alms.

It never entered the heads of these two women, any more than the head of little Margaret herself, that they, in giving birth to their boy and girl, had committed sin of which they should repent. Her offspring of shame has been to each woman the flower and crown of her life, the bright spot in her existence. The cup she has had to drink has been bitter enough; its one sweet drop has been mother-love. The boy and girl have grown to man and womanhood now; they are in middle life indeed, with the premature look of age upon them which characterises the very poor. Not an especially well-favoured couple, nor very gracious in bearing. One wonders, was all that love and labour lavished in vain? Would the world have been no worse place — better even, with so many mouths less to feed, so much room to spare for healthier, more promising members of the universal brotherhood — had those two babes of Hannah and Rhoda Lawrence been left to perish?

No question of this kind, thank God, troubles the feeble woman crouching over her fire, the busy woman at her ironing-board.

To the simple thinking of the gal La'rences, and compared with the semi-starvation of earlier days, the sisters live in affluence now. Their spotless, wholesome cottage is as a palace to the swarming grandchildren, offspring of the married cousins — that big-headed, small-limbed race, whose heated complexions and scaly skins render them of but small attractiveness in stranger eyes. Every meal partaken at the grandmothers' table is a feast. To sit on Sunday afternoons on the shiny chairs ranged round the walls, with an apple off the one apple tree in the garden and perhaps a chestnut apiece to hold in their hands, is a privilege which it would be terrible to forfeit. It is Hannah who presents the new pinafores; Rhoda whose hands, tortured by rheumatism, "blow up" as big as her head in her efforts to keep little stockings and elbows free from holes. That one among them whose turn it is to dine with the gal La'rences "come Sunday" is regarded for the time as the most enviable of mankind. There is no room for uncertainty about the fare; the unchanging Sabbath-day repast, laid forth on the white, coarse cloth of the little round table, is the same year after year: a tiny joint of cold baked pork, a large rice pudding in a yellow pie-dish, a basin of hot potatoes, and a wedge of cheese.

It isn't so much what there is to eat which fascinates the little visitor, perhaps, fills him with such unspeakable longing in anticipation, such rapture in enjoyment; it is the order, the cleanliness, the sweet propriety of all which appeal so strongly to the small grandchild. To see the black-handled knife and fork laid beside each willow-pattern plate, the white cup and saucer with the small blue flower (the gal La'rences always indulge in tea for the Sunday dinner); to admire the glass salt-cellar, the knitted mat adorning the plate which holds the loaf; to smell the wall-flowers in their jar among the precious ornaments on the side-table; to catch glimpses through the open door of the neat little flower-borders, the buttercup meadows, and blue fields of sky beyond — these are the things, after all, which make the Sunday festival memorable.

The boy "Biller" was little more than eighteen years of age when it was discovered to be advisable to marry him as soon as might be to his cousin of twenty-three.

"They'd been allus brought up, and slep' together as little uns — 'twere on'y nat'ral like," Rhoda says indulgently, telling the tale of the marriage. "It all come of Becker a-comin' home for the Whissun holidays. Biller, he'd growed 's w'uskers since she went awaay two yeer agone, and when she set eyes on 'm she set a-laughin'. That wos how it were — she set a-laughin'."

The explanation,which seems to be somehow deficient, is quite satisfactory to Rhoda. In talking to such simple people, the discrepancy between the picture in the mind's eye and its verbal exposition is very observable. It arises perhaps from a frequent talking over of facts in a small circle where the details are already known. It is probable that by an inhabitant of Dulditch a lively and lengthy history of courtship and marriage is at once unfolded by the allusion to the time when "Becker set a-laughin'."

But the consequence of this early marriage of Becker, who could never keep her places, and the boy who had not received "man's wage" long enough to have saved from his earnings was that the young couple had to go into debt to furnish their house, and have remained in difficulties to the present time.

The pair, struggling in extremest poverty, are given to look with a grudging eye upon the comforts of Hannah and Rhoda. Such spotless cleanliness has very much the air of luxury to Becky, worn out with an apparently hopeless washing of eight children and a continual scrubbing of an always fresh "drabbled" floor. Of that table of ornaments, presented principally by the "Rober'son child'un," for whose parents Hannah works — tiny baskets, in which sweeties had once been packed, empty chocolate boxes, sixpenny ornaments bought from the gipsy at the door, cracked wine-glasses — Becky is proud while resenting the splendid effect. With her house full of children she acknowledges that such elegancies would be inappropriate, even if attainable — there is barely room for the chairs to seat the numerous progeny in the over-crowded place; but the female soul longs after the ornaments of life, and the treasures are looked at with admiration, but askance.

It is matter of complaint between husband and wife that "mothers" could do more than is done for them all. Yet in this forbearance the women still consider their children, as they have always done. They have their own old age to provide for, the not distant time when the one working member of the little partnership can work no more. Their children are faultless, the most beautiful, wise, and affectionate of their species, but it will not do to "come on" Biller and Becker in a few years to support their respective mothers. The pleasure of helping son and daughter in their necessity is perhaps the greatest the women could experience; but it must not be indulged in, any more than those other pleasures of life which Rhoda and Hannah, did they give the matter a thought, must acknowledge they had known only to decline.

Should it come to pass that the maintenance of their mothers must fall upon Becker and Biller, the bread so eaten would be the bitterest of all the bitter bread the "gal La'rences" had eaten, would be washed down with the saltest tears. Had they not under their eyes the case of half a dozen old men and women, for whose support sons and daughters, compelled thereto by the parish, were contributing their hard-earned, ill-spared, dearly-grudged shillings? Was there not old Marthy Brown, for instance, whose eldest born, living only five miles off, had refused to see his mother for twenty years, so incensed was he at having to sacrifice a tithe of his income to maintain her? Was there not poor old

Skipper, continuing, to his sorrow and dismay, hale and hearty at nearly ninety years of age, spite of the wrong he was doing his children by keeping out of his grave?

"What! Yu bain't dead yit?" is the usual filial greeting to which the poor old fellow is accustomed.

"Well, I were the same to my faather," Skipper admits, mumbling the matter over to himself at his scant and lonely fireside — he does not complain.

But, rather than share the fate of Skipper and old Marthy, Hannah and Rhoda turn niggards to the clamorous horde about them, and store their hard-earned shillings with greediest care.

Another case they remember too: that of Shadrach Allen — he whose three sons, living in a distant county, were summoned to Dulditch to attend their father's death-bed. Shady, poor lonely old man, cheered up at the sight of those middle-aged boys of his whom he had not seen for a dozen years. The presence of those heavy, altered faces did him more good than "a hape" of medicine had done; the illness took a favourable turn. The doctor when he came laughed good-naturedly over his patient's improved condition, rallied the old man on having taken them all in, his medical adviser above the rest, and declared that Shady was "good enough man still to see out half the young uns."

His laugh was not echoed by the solemn-looking sons sitting in their Sunday clothes around the bed. The old man had been a burden on them for a good many years. They had come a "matter o' tew hunder' mile to see faather die; 'twould be middlin' awk'ard" if he failed to do what was expected of him.

But Shadrach did not fail. The sons took care he did not. They quietly ignored the doctor's altered tone; they did not recognise the improved condition of their parent. "He'd allust thort he'd git over this bout," the old man cheerfully declared. "'Twere along o' their bein' so good to 'm he'd made shift to drag along so far; and, please th' Lord, he'd git t'rough th' summer agin — th' summer that allust aised his corf and set 'm up wonnerful." The sons paid no heed to "sech-like mardlin"; their faces discouraged all hopefulness; they spoke to him only on the subject of his demise. They reminded him that they had procured a fortnight's holiday, thinking that that would see the finish of all things; they hoped the "p'or old man 'ud be out of ' mus'ry" before that time, please the Lord.

It was those sons of Shadrach, who had "holp" him with contributions of a shilling a week each for much longer than was agreeable to them, who nursed him to death. Their devotion was edifying in the extreme, and the neighbours all declared them to be "wonnerful 'fectionate young chaps". They would not let him put so much as an arm upon the coverlet, but kept the "twilt" pulled tight under Shady's nose; one or other of them was always employed in tucking it in tightly around him. They declined the proffered services of the next-door women to "shiffen"the old man in his bed, declaring "'twould be a sin to onsettle po'r old faather in 's last hours." It was not Shady who benefited by the port wine and the soup sent from the Rectory. "Th' old chap were past nourishin'," they said, and for days they persisted in giving him cold water out of a teaspoon as his only refreshment, other members of the family having taken that unstimulating beverage alone for the last days of their lives.

Well, they had "kep'" him in comfort while he lived, had "holp" him through his dying illness, and they closed his eyes when he died. Many times Shady had assured them from his strict retirement beneath the sheet that they had been the best of sons to him; and they conscientiously acquiesced in the statement. By hurrying the burying a little they were even enabled to follow the old man to his grave and to superintend the selling of his sticks of furniture before their fortnight's leave was up.

The doctor was a little surprised to find a corpse instead of a recovery on his next visit. He was somewhat abashed before the triumph of the sons, who "had seen death writ in 's faace from th' fust," they said. "We nivver had no other thort but that he were a goin'. We waited on 'm hand and fut, but we nivver, so to say, had no hope."

The man of medicine had thought otherwise, certainly; he had thought that by careful nursing and strict attention to his directions——. But it was not the first time the parish doctor had been mistaken by a good many. A few hours would bring about great changes, he admitted, and one could not give the close attention to the paupers' cases that perhaps they needed.

By that time the doctor's gig had whirled him to another "pauper case," and Shady's name was struck off his list and forgotten.

But Rhoda and Hannah Lawrence had no desire to be nursed out of existence in this attentive way, even by Billy and Becky.

"'Tis nat'ral," they say, "nat'ral th' young uns sh'ud feel th' old uns a barden." They are sorry for the parents, but they do not condemn the children. "'Tis but nat'tral."

And so most anxiously they apply themselves to the increasing of their little hoard. If good luck attend them and "th' Lord plaase," there is always the "chancet" that they may not survive the time when Hannah is too old to work. Then the son and the daughter will reap the benefit of those savings, a thought stimulating to yet further effort.

Hannah, what with her heaters and her starch and the difficulties with the bosoms of "the master's" shirts, is too much engaged for sustained conversation. But Rhoda, crouching over the bright fire, her swollen and cramped

... he gi'en us aich a pair o' butes.

hands lying idle perforce in her lilac apron, is "allust fit ter mardle, and allust wor," the sister declares, and adds that she "bain't a sayin' as how Rhoda were one o' them golderin' ones tha's allust a runnin' on; on'y companiony and agraable-like."

So Rhoda, while you will sit to listen, is glad to talk; and her favourite theme is of the days of their extremest poverty, when "bread and groshery was dare, and Becker and Biller wos little uns." She tells the story simply enough, with smiles rather than tears; with no thought that it is a tale of heroism — that she is revealing the history of a constancy and a courage of the highest and a devotion which is beyond praise and without reward. She tells it because, sitting there, racked with pain, crippled, a fixture in the chimney corner, she is proud to remember that she was once, as she says, "as good a man as Hannah." That she, too, morning after morning, turned out in the darkness, the biting wind and sleet to the day's work. That although, being a woman, she only earned sixpence a day, work as she might, she could yet fill a tumbril as quickly as the best man on the farm, could weed the "mangles," gather stones, top and tail the "turmits" as well as he.

"Th' maaster he complain sometimes there bain't no women nowadays to wark i' th' fiel's; but though the young uns is *nicer* than they wos in my day, 'tis maybe for the best," Hannah says, and glances at Rhoda's crippled limbs. "There's women that can stand such a life," she adds, with a sharp shake of the garment she is about to iron, "but then there's also women that can't."

When Becky was about five years old luck seemed suddenly about to change for the gal La'rences — only seemed, alas! And about this chapter of their simple history, opening so brightly and ending only in disappointment and woe, no word is said in Hannah's presence. Rhoda watches her opportunity, waiting till the elder sister goes into the little garden to collect the collars and small articles hanging out on the gooseberry bushes to bleach, or into the little inner kitchen to attend to the bread "doin'" in the "bak'us." The crippled sister gives you the story with her hand on your knee, her face pushed forward, in a hurried and husky whisper.

"He wor a stiddy, hard-warkin', 'dustrious chap, and he cast 's eyes on Hennah. He spoke her fair enough, and said as how he wanted a wife, and he ha'n't no 'bjections to me a livin' 'long on 'em nor yet to th' child'un. His mother, she were a foul-mouthed old mawther, and she come a mobbin'. 'I want nothin' to du wi' yu, Mis' Butters,' Hennah she up and say tu her, 'nor yet wi' none o' th' bilin' on yer, 'cept Jabez; an' I reckon he know 's own mind and want none o' yar interfarin'.' Hennah she'd got chakes like a pe'ny i' them days and eyes like sloes, and there weren't none on 'em that dust take no lib'ties wi' Hennah; and Jabez he' set 's heart on her.

"He were a-gettin' o' things comf'table for 's home, and Hennah she'd been cried i' th' chech, and 'twere i' th' haymakin' time. Me and Hennah, we wos a rakin' side by side — 'twere i' Rober'son's cherry-tree piece (Hennah she ha'n't niver so much as named the name o' that theer field up till this day) — and th' sun were molten hot. I were a'most done up. I looked at Hennah. 'Bor,' I say, 'how yu du swat.' 'I du,' she say; 'th' drops be a fallin' off on me like rain. Tha's bad for the men a mowin',' she say; and I knew as she were a thinkin' o' Jabez, for he were a fiery-hidded chap — like all th' Butters — wi' a short neck, and he felt th' hate won'erful.

"An' someone come a runnin' — 'twere a p'or du-nothin' mawther that ha' left the parush now, and right glad I were when she went, for the sight on 'er allust giv' Hennah a turn arter that day. She flung up her hand and kep' a calin' su'thin' acrost the swaths o' hay.

"We cou'n't make nothin' on 'er, and she kep' a callin'

still. Hennah she hulled down her rake and went up ter th' wumman. Then she come back and set a rakin' oncet more. 'Wha's come ter th' mawther?' I say tu 'er. 'Bor, he's dead,' she say. 'Jabez ha' fell down dead i' th hayfiel'.'

"Hennah she tuk 't wonerful quite-like. Like a sorft fule as I were I set a blubberin', but Hennah she di'n't imitate to make no complaint. 'That fare as ef I'd allust knowed it,' she say. 'I ban't one o' them to make a piece o' wark.'

"Yet Hennah weren't never th' same wumman arter that day's wark," Rhoda assures you. And then, perhaps, Hannah returns to the front kitchen and the ironing board, and Rhoda, to get as far as possible from that scene of the summer hay-making, plunges into a description of beet-pulling 'mid the snows and slush and sleet of winter.

"We used ter pull our pett'coats 'twin our legs trouser-fashion," Rhoda goes on, "and fine and mucky our stockin's got by night-time; and we allust had ter wash 'em out for th' morning', for we'd on'y a pair o' white uns apiece. An' then ol' master — we'd played along o' him when ' wos a buoy, and he allust tuk notus 'f me and Hennah — he gi'en us aich a pair o' butes. Wellinghams, he called 'em, and they was the usefullest iver yu see, for they come right up o' th'leg; and ef so be as yu ha'n't a pair o' stockin's on no one weren't th' wiser."

Then Hannah, engaged in testing a red-hot iron by holding it within half an inch of her cheek, declares with perceptible bitterness that Rhoda "shou'n't tell about them theer butes," and adds, as she brings the heater forcibly down upon its work, "We shou'n't nivver ha'had 'em ef so be as i'd ha' had my way."

Whereat Rhoda chuckles and explains that Hannah is always "s'naisty" on that subject, being of opinion that on that cold and rainy morning when "th' master" called over the hedge to know why Rhoda and Hannah hadn't got their buskins on, Rhoda, wet to the knees, standing among the drenched leaves of the turnips, should have answered with prevarication. She should, Hannah maintained, have perished ("paraged," she called it) sooner than "let on" that of buskins they had none.

"'Twere like askin o' th' man to give 'em," Hannah says with fierceness.

"But I wanted 'm ter give 'em," says Rhoda simply.

At which Hannah brings down her heater with force upon the sleeve of the nightdress lying spread before her. It is akind of protest against Rhoda's view of the subject. She has gone over the whole story so often in the last thirty years, there is no good in repeating her arguments; only——.

"Hennah, she were allust won'erful proud," Rhoda goes on, with visible pride of her own in that quality of "Hennah's". And she tells how, in the harvest field, when "th' 'levenses and fourses" came round, and the labourers' wives and children would bring their meals into the field, and the men, sitting in the midst of their own and their neighbours' families, would enjoy the extra delicacies appropriate to the occasion — the mild home-brew, the wedge of "mate dumplin'," the harvest cake — Hannah would ostentatiously set forth her slice of cheese upon the red handkerchief spread upon her knees, "as grand as the rest on 'em."

"'Twere for show on'y," Rhoda says, chuckling, and it lasted all through the harvest month. "Th' chase were for show only, and so 's none cou'n't pity us with our slice o' bread, or think as we was forced to it."

A white glass bottle of cold tea was also carried out day after day for appearance sake, the cold water which served them to slake their thirst disguising its tell-tale hue in a black bottle.

Hannah laughs a little shamedly over the reminiscence, bending the dark head, into which no line of white has come as yet, above the ironing-box upon which she is pressing with both hands.

"I di'n't want no hape o' talk," she explains. "They'd ha' been orferin' me their wittles; an' they'd ha' choked me."

Rhoda presently goes on to speak of one especial night when things had come to the worst. A week or so before a sister had died, leaving a child of six years old with no prospect before it but the workhouse. No "flesh and blood" of the gal La'rences had been "beholden" to the parish as yet; and without any hesitation, with no debate on ways and means, no question as to how the extra mouth was to be fed, such as must have agitated people less desperately poor, they walked one evening, work being done, to the parish where the mother had died and fetched the orphan home.

It was as much as they could do to keep life in the four of them without this added burden, for flour was half a crown a stone in those days, and if they worked every day of the week, which through stress of weather and other drawbacks they could not always do, there was only six shillings to take at the end of it. Out of this a shilling must be laid aside for rent and a shilling for the services of Happy Hunter, whose watery eyes used to gleam with delight for her part when she received the magnificent sum.

"I tell ye," Hannah says, "I was allust er'table in them times; but my wust tempered days wos pay-days. I were that worritted to know how to make it go th' fuddest."

But this especial evening was not that of pay-day, and things looked more than usually hopeless. The last slices of bread had been sent in the children's dinner-bags to school; the two sisters had had nothing but some raw turnip, eaten in the field, to stay their hunger since morning.

"We must git suffin' somehow to put inter our insides ter-night," Rhoda said, as they walked home through the winter evening's dusk.

But for once Hannah despaired. ("She were th' strongest, but she were allust th' downest-hearted," Rhoda explains.)

"We'd best ha' done with it, and give 't up," she declared. "Howsomdever I telled her we worn't sech downpins as that come tu yit," Rhoda continues. "We'd done to th' best o' our know, and now th' Lord 'ud ha' to help us. I dussen't say so to Hennah, but I'd up and arst Him tu, time we wos i' th' fiel'. For I'd been a tarnin' matters over, and I seen that, whether Hennah liked it or no, we must ha' help, ef so be as th' child'un worn't ter parage. An' when we got in, what d' yer think we see? A half-sack o' taters shot agin th' wall, and as much as a peck o' bewtiful inions, and a bushel or more o' apples! 'Twere a present from th' folk up to th' Hall, a neighbour telled us, to all them cottages as hadn't no gaarden.

"'Worn't I right?' I say to Hennah. 'I telled ye suffin 'ud turn up, and here be half a sack o' taters!'

"But Hennah, she were snaisty still: she were allust grudgin' agin anythin' she ha'n't, so to say, warked for.

"'A sight o' good taters be without no saucepun to bile 'em in!' she say.

"For our one was past mendin', at las', and we'd gi'en it awaay to a neighbour to mess up her chickens' food in, on'y the day afore.

"'I *'on't* let on we ha'n't no saucepun. I *'on't* ha' no borrerin', Hennah, she say. And so the end on 't were we biled th' taters i' th' kittle; and I don't know as iver I tasted none better biled, nayther."

And after supper Hannah, who was never a hand at thanking people, put the little ones to bed and scrubbed the floor, and "redd up" the kitchen, while Rhoda walked the couple of miles to the Hall to thank "th' laady" for her gift. And "th' laady," who was Sir Thomas's mother, "without no haughtiness about her,"came out of a room where "singin' and musickin' were going on bewtiful," and spoke to Rhoda herself, and ordered her a "glass of wind" and a slice of cake, and told her that out of some dozen families to whom like presents had been distributed among the cottagers, she had been the only one who had been gracious enough to say a word of thanks. After which she asked many questions and seemed interested in the answers; and she insisted on Rhoda taking home the remainder of the cake for the children, with some tea and sugar and a tin of rich soup for herself. "And a nice how-d'ye-du there were wi' Hennah for my a takin' of 'em!" Rhoda chuckles.

But the worst of the troubles of the "gal La'rences" were over after that night, for the Hall lady "tuk notus" of them and gave them sewing work to do — not very particular jobs at first, their hands being so stiff, and not enough of it to allow them to give up their field work. Many and many a night did Hannah, the day's work being done, sit sewing until the hour came round to begin the work of another day, Rhoda having been decoyed to her night's rest by the promise that Hannah would soon join her. But the women grew in favour with the Squire's wife, and presently the field labour was given up and the hard struggle was over.

They never, however, "tuk kindly ter th' sewin', bein' used to active employment," and the Hall lady being dead, and Rhoda fallen rheumatic, Hannah was glad to take the washing at Rober'son's, which she keeps to the present day.

The "Rober'son child'un" had most of them been born since she was there, and she'd seen some of them grow up and go out into the world, but she is "fond of 'em all," she tells you and "th' child'un is fond of me. As fur Rhoda — they'd allust come ter Rhoda in all mander o' little troubles — there'd allust been child'un in Rhoda's life, she were so wonnerful set on 'em."

Rhoda admits the soft impeachment and counts up her treasures for your benefit.

"Fust there wos Becker and Biller and po'r Arnust" (the dead sister's child). "He, po'r chap, had fell orf th' shaffs of a cart th' fust year he warked o' th' farm — an' he so proud o' arnin' his little wage — and were brought in with 's hid a mash and 's inside a gushin' out 'f 's body. Then there was the Rober'sons, bless their little hearts, and now th' gran'child'un that sometimes fared th' darest and most engagin' o' th' lot."

"Ef 'tweren't for me she'd allust have 'em messin' about," Hannah declares. "They smudder th' floor wi' their mucky butes, and allust a fingerin' and a fidgettin' — makin' a sight o' wark."

"Better so than to be as bad off as Sam Uttridge," Rhoda avers.

If you have not already heard the interesting history of Sam Uttridge, Rhoda will tell you that the gentleman in question is a nephew of theirs, who, being in every other way prosperous and commendable, labours under the extreme disadvantage in Rhoda's eyes of having been married for fourteen years to a wife who has not borne him a child.

Rhoda has on this account the deepest compassion for Mr Uttridge (his name, by the way, is Etheridge, but that does not make his case better or worse), the utmost contempt for his better half.

"To call herself a wumman! I wonder what she think women are made fur?" Rhoda cries, for she takes a very simple view of the great woman question which, unknown to her, is agitating so many superior minds, and she is happy in the proud consciousness of having fulfilled to her entire satisfaction her own mission.

If you inquire into Mrs Sam Uttridge's antecedents, you will hear that the lady is an "orficer's" daughter, and on pursuing inquiries you will learn that in the "gal La'rences'" vocabulary an "orficer's" daughter is not the child of a gentleman in the army or the navy, as might naturally have occurred to you, but of one whose occupation ("writin' and figgerin' and seck-like") lies in an office.

Was Margaret right, I wonder, and are these two women, crouching by the fire, toiling at the wash-tub, to be envied after all?

To me who write, to you who read, such a history is one of sordid, unrelieved misery, we say. But are we happier after all? We have loftier aspirations, higher ideals, nobler ambitions. But do we realise, can we attain them? We can only be successful in that which we put before us as the object to be accomplished. We can but have the thing we long for. In a world so filled with disappointment, where failure is for the many and success for the very few; where desire is so constantly baffled and hopes drop off before fruition; where thwarted ambition embitters the heart, and shattered illusions leave the eyes that beheld them darkened for ever; where the cravings of the soul seem given us only to be denied; where, grasping the thing we long for, we find it broken and ruined in our hands — in such a world surely the "gal La'rences" may esteem themselves blest.

For the one simple duty of their lives they fulfilled, the one uncomplicated desire of their hearts they attained to.

And, for that Biller and Becker — the unlovely, the loutish, the ungracious, and uncouth, whose births were shameful, whose personalities are disagreeable, whose histories are squalid — are born into the world, and are in their own obscure way holding their own there, the two women nightly give thanks and are ready at any moment to sing their *Nunc Dimittis*.

A DULDITCH ROSE

WITHOUT a word in anyone's ear Rosa Weeks started off one morning from her lonely cottage in Dulditch. With her thin lips tight-drawn, and the eyes, set deep in her sharp brown face, very bright and determined, she walked through the heat of a summer noon the four miles to the workhouse, and returning, brought with her the few weeks old orphan baby of which one of her sons had been the father.

"No child o' my flesh and blood shorn't be a work'us brat — not while I live, it shorn't — ef I starve for it," said Rosa Weeks.

So for her dead George's boy, in her old age, Rosa took up the burden of her youth again, going with half rations that the child might have bread, tearing up her poor stock of linen to make him clothes. The allowance she had from the parish — the weekly two shillings and half-stone of flour — was not sufficient to support the child as well as herself. Milk must be bought for the child. Therefore she bent her stiff back and strained her old limbs to labour again — to field work when she could get the work to do, to stone-picking, to acorn-gathering, when that was not to be obtained. A fierce old Ruth, she quarrelled and swore and fought among the gleaners once more, grabbing her own share and that of others where she could get it — for the sake "o' th' buoy."

"Th' buoy" the while, together with the sticks she had collected on the way, lying in the old green go-cart which had been the cradle of all her children; beneath him the bottle of cold tea, the slice of bread intended for refreshment in the pauses of labour.

When "th' buoy" was unusually refractory, a neighbour's larger baby would be hired at the price of her "wittles" and a ha'penny a day to "shug" the green go-cart while Rosa worked near by. For the boy, even at the earliest age, would never lie staring placidly at the sky overhead when he awoke, as would the more satisfactory babies of the class, but would kick and shout, and clamber up the side of the cart, and get wrong things into his mouth, and generally make his presence felt. It was the sun and the wind beating early and late upon his uncovered face which, added to his originally swarthy complexion and coal-black hair, gave him such a gipsy look perhaps. That, and the wandering glance of his wild dark eyes and the fashion of the garments in which Rosa clothed his early years.

It was a sight to make one laugh, or weep, to see little "Jarge" Weeks toddling off to school in his nondescript array. His tiny trousers made out of an old black and white large-checked shawl, which had for about forty years adorned Rosa's own shoulders; his coat fashioned from her dark green petticoat and cut in accordance with the exigencies of the petticoat shape; his hat of the same material as his trousers.

When Jarge attained to years of discernment he fought against that cap, taking pains to lose it in all sorts of irrecoverable places. But the parish of Dulditch could not hide the mongrel head-gear. It was as the actions of the just, which are said to survive and flourish under the most unkindly circumstances. It was like the ointment of the right hand which bewrayeth itself. Poor Jarge's abhorred millinery was, times beyond number, rescued and restored to him. It was stoned from the highest tree, picked out from the deepest "pit," sifted from the widest dust-bin. Grown desperate, the owner and a co-conspirator poked it under a "hape o' quicks" in one of "Rober'son's" fields, to which, having secreted a box of matches, they proceeded to set fire. But ill-luck attended this bold stroke also. The farmer appearing on the scene before the weeds were well alight, the delinquents scampered off, one only being recognised by the cap beneath the "quick" heaps. Poor Jarge went hungry, bruised, and sore to bed that night, thrashed, in addition to the many promiscuous thrashings which daily fell to his share, by particular request of the tyrant Rober'son.

When his troubles with his cap were past — for in a world given over to decay even Gran'mother Weeks' confections succumb at last — trouble was by no means ended for Jarge. Trouble and "th' buoy" were akin from birth, it seemed — trouble and restlessness and mischief.

It was he that stoned the ducks and chickens in the Brightlands farmyard (who was discovered in that act, rather, for everybody stoned them — to "hull a ston' and lame th' old gander," or to break the wing "o' th' old yiller hin," being considered by the youth of the neighbourhood a legitimate pastime and a praiseworthy attention to their employer's poultry); who ran the colts in the Fen; who infuriated the hitherto pacifically inclined bull "i' Rober'son's midder" till that animal, declining apparently to tackle his lawful prey, turned his unwelcome attention upon Betty Barker, going, can in hand, up to the farm for the "skim milk" which was her portion. The bull put down his head and bellowed so alarmingly at Betty that that comfortable old body must needs take to her heels and run, an exercise which brought on her "heart's disase" badly, compelling her to sit for an hour in the farm kitchen to have her courage revived and her palpitations lessened by doses of plum cake and beer. On her return journey she was accompanied by two sturdy champions, who, with sticks and stones and pitchforks, so infuriated the bull that he showed fight in earnest, and had to have a ring put through his nose, with a yard of chain dangling from it, at last.

It was Jarge who was the refractory boy of the school; who was always kept in for his own fault and that of other children during play and dinner hours; who threw a book in the mistress's face. It was he who took live mice in his trousers' pockets to church; whom the outraged clerk dragged up by the ear and set in the centre of the chancel steps, an awful warning to the congregation — some other boy having laughed aloud. It was Jarge — profane young rascal to whom nothing was sacred — who, coming upon the rector's little daughter gathering a lapful of the cuckoo flowers that whitened the lush herbage bordering the "dekes i' th' waater midder," chased that fleet-footed little maid homeward, catching her at last by the pollard-alder at the gate. The child struggled and fought and scratched in his arms. "Yu air a little buty, yu air, and I *wull* kiss yer, "Jarge declared, which feat he finally accomplished; and not all little Margaret's entreaties, nor all her tears, nor her passionate agonies of remorse, could save Jarge's skin from a hiding for that exploit.

For it was as that sweet time of year when "once more the Heavenly Power makes all things new," when the white thorn is at its prime, and the cuckoo is shouting in the woods; and Margaret's big brother, home from his first term at college, was lying flat on his back at no great distance from the alder, staring up to the fleecy white clouds sailing over the blue. It was the vigorous arm of the parson's son that saw to the dusting of master Jarge's jacket on that occasion.

"It wasn't that I minded his kissing so much," Margaret sobbingly informed her avenger when the beating was over and she and her brother had turned their backs on the offender, lying stretched at his full length beneath the alder, his arms above his neck, his face buried deep in the grass; "it was that his jacket smelt so funnily."

That patchwork, queer-fashioned little jacket of his was always coming into contact with the correcting rod. Rosa's "buoy" was the "scorge" of the parish, it was allowed on all sides, and heavily the "scorge" was "scorged" — without that improvement accruing from such drastic measures as Solomon has led us to expect. The wicked light did not die out of Jarge's wandering black eyes, nor did his "anticking" cease.

It was out of respect for his grandmother alone that "Rober'son up to the faarm" hired the youth, on his leaving school, at the wage of three shillings a week, to "plough and to sow, to reap and to mow, and to be a farmer's boy." All the neighbours remarked that better days were coming for Rosa at last, and that Jarge would now have a "chanet" of making a "man i' th'warld."

But only disaster followed this propitious commencement. Jarge jammed the tips of his fingers in the cake-crusher, broke his ankle through dangling his legs among the machinery of the chaff-cutter, was caught in the act of stealing eggs in the waggon lodge. On one occasion, being entrusted with a gun for the frightening of crows in the young barley, he carried it home, and in the dusk of the spring evening discharged it through the keyhole of his grandmother's neighbour's door. And thereby did Jarge set fire to the shawl which hung over that door to keep the draught out, and frighten old Maundy Harper till her "inside was all of a trimble," as she declared. Furthermore, having been enrolled a member of the Juvenile Band of Hope — thanks to the attraction of a teetotal tea in the schoolroom — it was Jarge who was brought home on the same evening dead drunk, and laid at his grandmother's door. "Meelyer Sprite's Arnest" had "dared him" to drink the mixture which had wrought his undoing, he explained later on. To do what he was dared to do was the beginning and end of Jarge's creed of honour.

Through all, although Rosa had set her face grimly, and laid on lustily with tongue and stick, she did not lose her love for "th' buoy" nor her faith in him; she did not hesitate to chastise him heavily for every crime, authentic or otherwise, laid to his charge, but she made a mortal enemy of that one who carried in such reports to her. Her life must have been but an uneasy one through all those years, for, the urchin once out of sight, she never could have known an instant's peace.

Every day as the time for his return from school, from play, from work, came round, Rosa, a shawl flung over her head to protect it from the rain, a brown hand held before her eyes to shield them from the sun, would stand at the garden gate looking anxiously up and down the road. Her lips would be always moving, for Rosa has the bad habit of talking to herself. Ten to one in passing her you would catch amid her whispered mutterings some word about "th' buoy."

For th' buoy's sake she fought against all the ills that attack old women — against feebleness, weariness, illness even.

Once, in the days when that historic cap and the small trousers of the large check were newly-fashioned, Rosa was smitten by her old enemy the "browntitus," and a more than usually serious illness laid her low. It seemed to those who looked in upon her, "to du the p'or ol' mawther a han's tarn" as she lay upon her bed, that she must succumb. They impressed that fact upon her after the unvarying fashion of such bedside comforters.

"Rose, bor — p'or ol' dare, yer a-dyin'; yer hour's come, bor. Don't set yerself agin it, nor fly i' th' Lord's faace."

Rosa flung up a touzled grey head from the pillow; her nightshirt, torn open at the throat to assist the difficult breathing, showed all the lean brown bosom; her fury gave her strength.

"I ain't a-dyin'," she cried fiercely. "Th' Lord! — what d'ye think th' Lord's arter, then, to taak me when th' buoy's a wantin' on me ivery tarn. Whu's to see arter th' buoy, ef so be as I'm tuk? Darn yer — I 'on't die, I tell yer I 'on't!"

And she didn't.

Jarge, grown tall enough, it was, who used to thrash his grandmother, the neighbours said, paying back all those chastisements of his boyhood with interest. It was allowed on his behalf that, much as he owed the old woman, he had "a sight" to put up with. For, originally a clean and tidy body enough, her sight failing her as time went on, dirt accumulated apace in Rosa's once wholesome little domain. On floors and walls and furniture and clothing it accumulated, and became mixed with the food, and encrusted on the saucepan and frying-pan, and ingrained in the sheets and table-cloths.

In spite of the corrective chastisements from Jarge, the sight grew worse instead of better, the dirt increased, so that the shirt laid out for "th' buoy" against he wished to "shiffen hisself" of a Sunday morning was as black as that he "t'rew off" on the Saturday night; so that the bacon dumpling prepared for the young man's principal meal, made in a dirty basin, boiled in a filthy cloth, served on a table-cloth which had been used by mistake to wipe the floor, was not exactly an appetising meal.

Small wonder if such food had a bad effect on Jarge's temper as well as on his stomach. But he was kind to his grandmother too, getting up to wait on her at night if she was restless, or her cough was bad; except for occasional outbreaks of temper, putting up with her sharp tongue and her villainous cooking with more patience than a good many better men might have shown.

Meanwhile his character as a labourer, as a member of a peaceful and law-abiding community, did not improve. He was dismissed from "Rober'son's," taken on, dismissed again. Having some real or fancied cause of complaint against his fellow-workman, Ben Pitcher, he waylaid the man one night as he returned from the "White Hart," where both had been drinking, tripped him up, kicked him into insensibility, and left him by the side of the road. Then, having at last made Dulditch too hot to hold him, Jarge took himself off, and for years none of us knew his whereabouts or what had become of him.

Rough attempts were made on all sides to console the grandmother. She was "well rid o' bad rubbage," she was told. "Th' buoy were allust a mucky chap," who would come to the "gallers as sure as nothin'." But Rosa was but a "snaisty" old woman even in her sorrow, and did not make polite replies to her Job's comforters.

"They wos all agin th' buoy," she muttered to herself, sitting in the loneliness of her now nearly total blindness, nose and knees together over her little scrap of fire, that tiny chair which had been little Jarge's, and Jarge's father's before him, pulled up close to her side. "All agin 'm! an' kep' a pesterin' o' me wi' all mander o' lies. But th' buoy were a good buoy, that he wor! He were gone awaay to git wark, but he'd come back, sure enough. Th' buoy'ud come back!"

We heard rumours in the course of time that Jarge had enlisted. But it was not till after several years that there came a letter from him in India to his grandmother, telling how he was sick of a fever, but was going to kill the "niggers" when he was well enough; and how, that pleasant duty being accomplished, he should come back to see the old lady once more.

The letter was full of the terms of endearment and the pious phrasing inevitable in the letters of the poor — was, in fact, a "butiful letter," as the neighbours all agreed. Many a score times it was read to Rose, who, when no one with learning enough for the task was by, strained her own nearly blind eyes over the worn and crumpled paper — Rose, who never had read a written word in her life! — restoring it always to that place between her soiled dress and her dirty stays where, since her blindness, all her treasures had accumulated.

"He's a good buoy, and I allust knowed it," she muttered as she folded the precious missive in her trembling brown hands. "Folks was agin 'm, but he' a good buoy, an' he's a comin' back."

Meanwhile Rosa, her house and all that was in it growing dirtier and dirtier, the attention of the relieving officer was called to the state of things. There came a Tuesday morning when, instead of her two shillings and her half-stone of flour, she received that dreaded official invitation which is conveyed in "an order for the house."

Then arose in that corner of Dulditch a commotion, the like of which has not been heard before. "Old Rose to go to th' work'us. Rose Weeks that had warked her fingers to th' bone, p'or old mawther, while she'd eyes left in 'r hid ter see. 'Twore a shame — a cryin' shame!" the other old women said, watching the relieving officer cross the road to Rosa's cottage, being very careful he did not overhear.

This official is cordially disliked and feared in Dulditch, for he has not a gentle or conciliatory manner, and those in receipt of relief credit him with a power he does not possess, putting down every unpopoular measure of those in authority to the account of this agent. Go where he may, this red-faced, loud-voiced servant of the guardians is not regarded as exactly a favourite; but wherever his not very pleasant duty may have called him, to the performance of whatever ungrateful task, he could not have been assailed with more violent and reprehensible language than that with which Rosa greeted him now. She, for one, had no fear of him. Of what in all her sturdy struggle for life had that unflinching soul of hers been afraid?

Powley is a big and burly man, but he beat a hasty retreat from that dirty cottage. Rosa, stumbling over the threshold, pursued him down the little path between the gooseberry bushes, pouring forth a stream of language which would not have disgraced the mouth of the proverbial trooper.

Rosa would not go to the workhouse; she would die of starvation, she would rot in a ditch before she was dragged there! We all knew it well. All her life she had talked of the extreme measures to which she would resort sooner than become a "porpoise." As year by year the hated fate had seemed to loom nearer and nearer her resolution had strengthened. And now, added to all that natural and acquired distaste, was this further consideration: if she was not at the cottage, waiting there for him, what, when at length he came home, was to become of "th' buoy"?

For the present, at any rate, the necessity against which Rosa has set her face is averted. The magnificent allowance from a grateful country, proud to help all brave, independent souls to carry on the fight of existence in the best of all possible worlds, is graciously continued. Nay, in that great country's regard for the well-being of an aged daughter of the soil, even an extra shilling a week has been provided wherewith to reward those neighbours who assist Rosa in her efforts to prevent the dirt, in which she lives, moves, and has her being, from quite overpowering her.

And Rosa quarrels with and swears at those neighbours who "come a-meddlin' along o' her." She loudly accuses them of robbing her linen-chest and her larder. They are poor enough to, those good women, but the slice of perspiring yellow cheese upon which the sugar and the candle-dripping are impartially spilt, the dirty wisps of nightcaps, and the yellow-hued rags appropriate to various uses, could hardly tempt the poorest.

Meelyer Sprite, in spite of a strong desire on her part to annex the weekly shilling, had to relinquish the post of "redder-up" for Rosa, or murder would have been done.

"Meelyer were allust a light-fingered mawther," Rosa says,

talking her over dispassionately now that she has successfully routed the lady in question. "Bor, I nivver could abide 'er, th' best o' times. I'd a sight suner be smuddered wi' muck than ha' that hussy imitatin' to fye out my plaaces for me."

So the neighbours "lend a han'," as they say among them, and, like all work that belongs to no one in particular, the business is not very well done. From Powley, great in dread authority, threats now and again come.

"You'd be best in the 'House,' old lady," he calls out to her, not unkindly, stopping his gig for a moment at her door on a Tuesday morning. "I shall have to get you an order for the 'House'."

Rosa, rage in her sightless eyes, comes, stumbling in her haste, to the door, shakes a threatening fist in the direction of the voice, and curses the relieving officer, loud and deep. Powley, safe in his gig, gives a chuck to the reins lying on his knee and laughs as he rides away.

Yet if she does not go to the workhouse what in saddest earnest is to become of Rosa? She is no longer able to pick up the sticks over which she and her neighbour Maundy have been wont to quarrel so bitterly. Maundy's stack grows bigger and bigger; she is queen of the situation at last. But Rosa's coal bill, although she puts on each atom of fuel grudgingly with the fingers with which she is mixing her flour or breaking her bread, cripples her resources. She cannot see to glean the ears of corn; she can no longer earn a sixpence by going an "arrand" for a neighbour, nor by tending a neighbour's child. Starve as she does, she cannot pinch her stomach enough to make up the three pounds needed for rent "come" Michaelmas Day. If she can't pay rent she must turn out. Where to go? The shadow of that hated inevitable refuge of the worthy and the worthless agricultural poor draws nearer and nearer upon Rosa's horizon every day.

But Rosa herself has no fear. "Wild horses 'on't drag me

theer" is all she says; repeats, perhaps, when pressed about her plans for the future, that she can "allust die in a ditch."

So we pass her, standing at her cottage gate — the staunch old soul who has made her brave fight and who is not beaten yet. She is not of those whose "feet and head come together in life's pilgrimage"; her slight, skinny figure is still upright as a dart. The grey hair, with its untidy, crooked parting, is blown away from the dark, sharp face with its thousand wrinkles. The brown eyes are sightless, but they are bright still, and turn with an eager watchfulness down the tree-shadowed road — the road that leads past the school. Those same eyes used to gaze anxiously down that chequered path of sunshine and of shade in the days when Jarge was the bad boy of the village.

She is waiting for him still.

Oh, Jarge, Jarge in India! When the shades of night come on and give you pause in that occupation of "nigger" slaying, with which in Dulditch we believe you to be so fully engaged — Jarge, the truant, the liar, the incorrigible, the hopeless — do you never, as you lie upon that bed you have made for yourself, tossing, fevered and sleepless, in the sweltering night, do you never see that road with the shadow of the palm-leaved chestnut branches moving over the sunlight; do you never see that withered, small figure waiting, patient, faithful, undoubting, by the cottage gate, muttering incessantly to herself of "th' buoy" so long in coming?

Since the above was written that question of Workhouse versus Death in a Ditch has, in Rosa Week's case, been settled by an Agent who arranges such-like difficult matters for us now and again.

Rosa made desperate efforts, but she must have failed. Heroically she pinched that poor old body of hers, denying it the warmth and food it needed, but that enormous sum of three pounds needed against Michaelmas Day could never have been saved by such means. She must have failed, but that "Heavenly Death" which provides for all saved her that bitter defeat.

The battle she fought all through her long life is over for Rosa, thank God. She stands no longer at the garden gate; the door of the cottage she loved is locked; the key will be given to her landlord together with what had been secured for Rosa's rent when on the eleventh of October he comes to claim his dues. The women who undressed her when she was dead found the little screw of shillings and pence tied to her filthy stays.

So God rest you, Rosa Weeks! Not realising how hard the struggle was, you fought a brave fight. Never once naming the name of duty to yourself, your duty was nobly done. Against your name may be written the words "mortua est," which, being interpreted, may be taken to mean in your case, Rosa, that your work being nobly done, you have earned your discharge.

THE LOST HOUSEN

ON the high road, a couple of miles from the village of Dulditch, but yet within the boundary of that parish, in the midst of a plot of garden ground all waste and uncultivated, the ruins of the two cottages stand which were known to the countryside by the above designation. The position of the "Lost Housen" is very lonely and remote from any dwelling. They are divided by the acre and a half of ground in which they stand from the wood which runs at the back and on one side of them; on the other side is an osier-bed, and beyond that the river; in front runs the road, from which a straggling, untrimmed hedge all but hides them.

Some forty years ago on the same site stood the turnpike lodge, and the place is still believed to be haunted by the ghost of the gate-keeper, brutally murdered in his bed by a tramp in the midst of the silence and darkness of a winter night. His body, dragged round the osier-bed, was found next morning in the river, too shallow even at that time of year to conceal the ugly crime.

For years after the last toll had been paid on the Runwich Road, the gate removed, and the lodge fallen to decay, the site remained unoccupied, owing to the loneliness of the situation, to the dampness of the surroundings, to the spirit of the murdered lodge-keeper hovering where the vapours lingered among the shivering osiers or rising mist-like from the river.

It was not until old Ambrose Crouch, the Dulditch blacksmith, died, leaving his few pounds of savings between his two sons, that the building of the two hideous cottages, which at present occupy the position of the old toll-house, was begun.

The tale goes that the blacksmith, having enjoyed several years of married life without issue, and being anxious for a couple of strong sons to help him in his trade and to save the wages of journeymen, made a bargain with the Almighty (whose name was familiar in his mouth more in cursing than in prayer) that if He would give him a pair of male children, Ambrose for his part would see to it that they bore respectively the longest and the shortest names in the Bible. When, within the year, Mrs. Crouch presented her husband with twin boys, those poor unconscious infants were accordingly burdened with the names of Og and Maher-shalal-hash-baz to carry through life.

Thus cruelly handicapped from the beginning, the race of life run by the two sons, for whom old Ambrose, after his ignorant and superstitious fashion, had prayed, was far from being a creditable one. Only Og, after all, helped his father to beat the sparks from the glowing iron in the forge, to shoe the cart-horses, lifting huge, unflinching hoofs for the operation, standing patient on the little green before the blacksmith's door. For anger in the Crouch family was apt to wax as hot and as dangerous as the great bars the men handled so unconcernedly amid the leaping flames, and words of rage and cursing sounded often above the ringing blows of the hammer on the anvil; and Maher — it was by this comparatively insignificant appellation that the owner of the formidable baptismal title was known in Dulditch — who was of a quiet and timid disposition, slipped away from the paternal roof one evening and did not return.

He only went as far as the next village, where he addressed himself to the profession of bricklaying, the noise and the heat of the blacksmith's work being repugnant to him; but it was very seldom afterwards that his father set eyes on the still, white face, the strange-looking blue eyes, the sleek, black hair of his truant son.

In those days the rural population was more averse even than at present from movement. Among the more old-fashioned of them one hears continually still of sons who for twenty years have not seen mothers living a few parishes distant; of sisters within walking distance who never meet. A man who lives within a hundred yards of the workhouse was overtaken the other day by the doctor of that institution, who, knowing the pedestrian, pulled up to ask him why, on working day, he was attired in his Sunday suit, and whither he was bound with such a determined gait.

"I'm a goin' to see faather," the man said. "'Tis a matter o' twanty year come th' thutty-fust o' next month sin' I sot eyes on th' old chap last. He be a gettin' along i' yares now; and me and my missus ha' set a wonderin' how 'e fare. So I ha' tuk a holiday and rid myself up, and I be a goin' to make my moind aisy by a glint on 'm at last."

The doctor, having sympathised with the somewhat tardy filial anxiety, offered a seat in his gig to help the pilgrim on his road, an honour the pilgrim, however, declined; and, with evident surprise that the whereabouts of "faather" was not universally known , pointed across the way to the big white poor-house, intimating that unlovely edifice as his destination.

He had lived within a stone's-throw of the miserable old pauper father for a score of years without feeling the impulse to cross the road to see him.

So Ambrose Crouch had only the one son and the wife to curse at, to batter with hard words and cruel blows. The mother was a woman slow of tongue, with eyes like Maher's, dull and blue as his, and with the same still gaze. How she aroused her husband's fury is not known; it is said that she never attempted retaliation. As for Og, he also seemed to be cowed by the fierce old man, and took his brother's portion of oaths and stripes as well as those due to himself with apparent resignation.

But the day came when the weakness of old age and illness robbed the tyrant of his power, and then did Og and his mother show of what material they were made.

"Th' po'r ol' chap were a bad ol' warmint, but he were th' best o' th' lot, arter all," the neighbours said, and said truthfully. For his sins he suffered terribly now. There was never a blow that was not paid back to him with interest; he was starved; he was terrified; he was tortured. He escaped from his bed once at noonday, and, in his night-shirt, ran about the village imploring the neighbours to take care of him and protect him. Old Brose Crouch was more terrifying in his frantic dread and in that scant attire than ever he had been in the height of his splendid strength and his unrestrained passion, cursing and swearing and wielding his mighty hammer at the forge. The women hid away from him, doors were slammed in his face.

Finally he was captured by wife and son and taken back to his bed again. Og pushed him homeward in a wheelbarrow, abashed and beaten, the poor old bare legs dangling helpless. The woman stalked before, silent, her thin lips drawn inward, the great pale blue eyes gazing into vacuity, by no means discomposed at forming one in such a procession.

Life was strong in the miserable old man. Starvation, exposure, ill-treatment of all kinds failed to kill him. He was found lying insensible upon the snow in his front garden early one morning. His head was cut and bruised, his arm and leg were broken; yet even then he did not die at once, but lived long enough to swear before witnesses that he had fallen from his window in his sleep, and that his son, who had ever treated him with kindness and attention, had had no hand in the disaster.

But the nearest neighbours had heard a cry for mercy in the night; there were signs of a struggle in the bedroom. The village people, excited by the presence of the police among them and athirst for a tragedy, insisted that Og Crouch should at once be taken to Runwich Gaol and hanged there. To their intense disappointment the culprit got off with a six months' imprisonment for assault, the father protesting his son's innocence to the last, dying —fortunately for him — just before that son's release.

Those cottages the blacksmith and the bricklayer undertook to erect with some of their father's savings were long in the building. The men were suspicious of interference in the work, and from foundation stone to topmost bricks in the chimney did everything themselves. Consequently in architectural design, in beauty, and in finish the "lost housen" left much to be desired. Before paint or paper or whitewash was put on the walls, the brothers, tired of the expense of lodgings, had moved into that cottage which they meant to occupy, and amid the squalid confusion of the miserable place had installed their mother to keep house.

Perhaps it was not to be expected that such a trio should live in peace. It was soon abundantly evident which one among them meant to be master. On the shoulders of Og, it seemed, his father's mantle had fallen. He swore at and beat his mother, cursed and fought his brother to his heart's content. The fear that Jemima Crouch had never shown of her husband she exhibited in a marked degree now of her son. She had seen him grow from childhood to middle age; she knew so much of him, she knew nothing that was not terrible. In her dread of Og Jemima drew near to the son who was so like herself in outward seeming — possessing the same tall, stooping figure, the same air of stillness and reserve upon the white, well-featured face, the same blue eyes, which never lit up, but gazed with their indescribable look into space.

If Maher sympathised with his mother's fears, or felt them on his own account, is not known. He was sparing of speech to an extra-ordinary degree, and his attitude was ever that of defence rather than defiance. He received what Og dealt out to him in food and fisticuffs, although his own share in the little patrimony had been equal with his brother's, and in spite of the fact that, physically, he was better made and far stronger, with long arms and enormously strong hands, which were quite equal to the task of retaliation.

Having once settled down in the miserable half-finished place, through whose single-brick walls the wet oozed and the wind blew, Og delayed to enter upon the finishing touches which should have made the home habitable. He guarded the remnant of the money carefully, carrying it on his own person night and day. They could live very well without paint on the "win-skirtin'" and the "windies," he declared. What was the good of whitewash or wall-paper while the "chimney" smoked, as he put it forcibly, "like hell"? Jemima, who had been used to a particularly neat and, for her class, even luxurious home in her husband's time, groaned with rheumatism and shivered with ague all the winter through. What Maher could do without outlay of capital for materials he did, but surreptitiously and in a half-hearted way. He cut wedges of wood to stop the rattling of the windows, and daubed a trowelful of mortar over the chinks in the chimney through which the smoke poured. But the effort needed to bring the outer door into closer connection with the doorstep was apparently too great for him, and in the work of cultivating the garden he never got further than spitting meditatively upon the soil over the spade upon which he leant.

Since the money had come into their possession the idea of adding to it by earning a day's wage had been abandoned by both the brothers. Og, who, as has been said, carried the purse, spent his days at the nearest public-house, where he drank himself ever into a savager, more brutal condition; while Maher sat silent with his silent mother, or roamed about the miserable place with his hands in his pockets, making a melancholy survey of its deficiences.

Then Og fell ill, the cold and the damp telling first on him, apparently the strongest of the three. He began with bronchitis and went on to inflammation of the lungs and to "ammonia"; and being a hard drinker upon whom the necessary stimulants took no effect, he lay very quickly at death's door.

On the fifth day, when the doctor came out of the bedroom, where a paraffin lamp, sending forth a most abominable stench, burnt day and night in a feeble struggle against the damp and chill of the place, he stopped to speak to Maher, sitting idle and alone in the living-room, his hands in his trousers pockets, his long legs, reaching nearly to the opposite wall, stretched before him, his blue eyes fixed vacantly.

"This brother of yours is in a very critical state, my man," the doctor said, pausing in the act of screwing his clinical thermometer into its case. "His temperature is a hundred and seven this morning. If that temperature be maintained till evening he will die."

Maher's eyes wandered slowly to the doctor's face and fixed themselves there for a long minute before he spoke.

"And if 't don't?" he asked at length.

"If the temperature declines, and the little strength the man at present has is maintained, there is a chance for him — he may recover. The next few hours will decide. I am sorry to tell you that in my opinion he is far more likely to die — and that quickly — than to live."

The young man said nothing. His eyes continued to be fixed on the doctor's face. There was something disagreeably fascinating in that long silent stare. What an odd-looking figure the man was, with his white complexion and in his white workman's dress! There was no play of expression in the face; the features were as emotionless and as still as those of a dead man.

"That old woman always gives me the creeps," the doctor said to himself with irritation, thinking of Jemima Crouch, sitting silent, gaunt, and upright by the bedside; "her son is as bad."

"I ha' heared the folk let on," said Maher, speaking slowly, with his hushed and far-off voice, "as how when a man lay at th' p'int o' death — his breath, which in an or'nary way he live by, a lavin' on 'm — I ha' heared say at them times the breath 'f a livin' human critter brathed into 's nost'ils and down 's tr'ut — ef so be as sech can be found as 'll go t'rough with' 'casion — 'ull bring that feller-suff'rer back from 's mortial plight."

Maher's rare speech was slow and difficult, and by the time he had reached the end of it the doctor had put away his thermometer, had buttoned his great-coat, had settled his hat on his head.

"And what," he asked as he drew on his driving gloves, "what do you supose your patient would be doing while you were whistling into his nostrils and blowing down his wind-pipe?"

"What?" Maher asked, having paused to watch the other button his gloves and turn to depart.

The doctor turned round upon him, the outer door in hand.

"Why, he'd be kicking the bucket, my good fellow," the cheerful doctor said with a laugh. "By the time you'd cured your man he'd be as dead as Moses."

Then he went, and Maher sat for long hours over the smoky fire, and gazed and gazed at the opposite wall.

At night Mrs Crouch always gave up her post in the sick-room to Maher, she repairing to her own bed for a few hours' rest. The mother and son stood for a few minutes over the fire before going their several ways.

"How du 'e fare?" Maher asked.

"Better," she answered. "To my thinkin' he ain't i' th'

chechyud yit. He be a goin' to live."

Maher's jaw fell open, his dull, mournful eyes widened; he said nothing, but gazed stupidly upon his mother. She, for her part, gave her report with nothing of that trembling joy with which a mother might be expected to welcome her son back from the grave.

"He be asleep," she said, "and his breathin's reg'lar. The pantin' and the ruttlin' on his chist 's left 'm. So 've the burnin' faver left 'm. He's all of a sweat."

She sat down, with a groan for her aching bones, in the chair Maher had vacated, and her strange eyes fixed themselves miserably upon the hot wood-ashes in the grate. Og objected to the expenditure for coal, and they burnt what bits of wood they found about the place.

"'Tis all to begin over agin," she said, whispering the words to the fire, leaning forward over her folded arms. "He's managing" (manageable) "in 's ways now, t'rough his wakeness, but give 'm 's strength, and we've a worse devil among us agin than iver 's father were — a cru'ler, selfiger, dartier-mouthed devil."

"Th' doctor let on as he were a goin'," Maher reminded her slowly.

"Ah!" she said. A quavering, long-drawn "Ah!" that expressed a great deal — her contempt of the doctor's opinon, her better knowledge of her son's condition among other things.

"We shall ha' to give 'm back the money agin," Maher said reflectively.

She only nodded at the fire, rocking herself to and fro over her folded arms.

Maher contemplated her in one of his long silences.

"We han't done it yit," he said at length with more than usual emphasis. "Maybe we shorn't ha' to du 'it arter all."

With that he turned away from his mother, and walked with something of decision in his shambling step into the adjoining room to take up his watch over the invalid.

Before the doctor started on his rounds on the following morning he received a message to the effect that his presence was not needed at the "Lost Housen," Og Crouch having died in the night. The man of medicine had left direction with Mrs Crouch that, in this too probable termination of the case, word should be sent him, as the cottage was out of his way; and he now signed the death certificate with a light heart and an easy conscience. He had a patient to see at a distance of fifteen miles in the opposite direction, and the weather was particularly bad that morning, so that the good man was glad to shorten his rounds.

"That shambling half idiot, his brother, didn't try his famous recipe for putting breath into his respiratory organs, I suppose?" he inquired jocosely of the messenger, the Dulditch carpenter, who had already measured the big blacksmith for his coffin, and who had volunteered to let the doctor know of the death. The man did not understand the allusion, and had it explained to him amid much chuckling on the doctor's part.

By night all Dulditch knew the story — how Maher Crouch had tried to save his brother's life by breathing down the dying's man's throat.

The experiment had been tried before in the memory of one or two of the villagers, not with success in any case, it seemed.

Gentleman George Ganders was full of information on the point for the benefit of the neighbours who passed his gate, his housekeeper Queenie Mask's mother's uncle having been operated on in like fashion when at his last extremity. Gentleman George related the occurrence with bated breath, for a "cur'ous thing had happened on the 'casion, as Queenie, who was a 'quite' body and didn't want no pace o' work made, had let on — a won'erful cur'ous thing." The dying uncle, Jabez by name, so it was told in the family, had rejected the breath so liberally offered in his hour of need, and had breathed his own "sperrit" down Uncle Thomas's t'rut, the consequence being that Uncle Thomas had never been "hisself agin" in any sense of the word, Jabez's "sperrit," after a sharp contest with the former inhabitant of the body, having at length "hulled out th' sperrit" of Thomas. So that the living man grew, even in outward form, the "moral" of the dead brother; and when asked, in the doubt of his identity naturally engendered in the family's mind, which of the two he was, had always unhesitatingly responded "Jabez".

"Th' wumman Queenie don't want no hape o' talk made on 't, as that happ'd 'n har own fam'ly; but that were the long and th' short on 't as she gi'en th' account to me. An' I take it 'tis a wonnerful p'or look on for Maher, according'," Mr Ganders said.

After such a precedent it is not very surprising that in Dulditch great interest was felt in the case of Maher Crouch, and a curiosity doomed to remain unsatisfied. Those who caught a sight of the man reported him as looking whiter than ever, which was not satisfactory to the prevalent expectation, for Og had inherited the ruddy complexion of his father. But all admitted that he had a "wonnerful cur'ous look" about the eyes. Asked to describe the look, they said it was "kind o' wild like." Now as Og had been always spoken of as a "wild chap" since his father's death, it was decided that "Og's sperrit was looking out of Maher's eyes," and the rustic mind was gratified.

Those who had seen Maher had penetrated to that miserable living-room where he and his mother sat silent over the fire at the mercy of the volumes of smoke that poured down the chimney; of the wind that blew in by cranny and crevice and whirled about them; of the rain that flowed under the door, and ran down the inside of the window, and trickled from the walls. For, in the light of day Maher Crouch never again stirred abroad. When the shades of night came on, his long figure, white and ghost-like in his bricklayer's jacket, might be seen sometimes, creeping about among the mists that rose from the osier bed, wandering around the uncultivated space that was to have been the garden of the brothers' domain. At the sound of a passing foot-fall, at the approach of wheels, he would, even in the darkness, hurry away to hide; for the silent unsociable ways of the man had, since his brother's death, developed into a determined shunning of his kind.

What sort of life the mother and son led together was only a matter of conjecture in Dulditch. Mrs Crouch, who had been "wonnerful shut-up and quite-like" always, and had made no friends among her neighbours, was shyer than ever of acquaintances, and had acquired since her son's death a nervous and suspicious manner, which those few people who succeeded in getting speech of her greatly resented. It is held to be mannerly in Dulditch for a woman to be as open-minded in her trouble as her joy. She should have no secret recesses in her mind — all the chambers should be thrown open, frankly and confidingly, to the friendly inquisition. There is nothing found so efficacious to ease the heartache as the popular expedient of having half a dozen women in to talk the matter over. One who refuses this form of consolation sows a grudge against her in the breast of her more generous-minded sister.

So it came to pass that in time the inhabitants of the "Lost Housen" were regarded as an unneighbourly, ill-conditioned couple, and were left to their own silent and secret devices.

No one quite knew when Maher Crouch disappeared from the scene. It was rumoured that the mother was living alone long before it was definitely ascertained that her son had left her. And even when the fact became established, no one could make out to his satisfaction where or why the man was gone. That their life together had been most miserable all firmly believed; but there was division on the point of whether he or she had been the "ill-condition'est." Nothing more wretched than the white, scared face of the mother could have been imagined till the wild, ashen face of the son had been seen. A man that never smoked "a pipe o' baccy," leaning over his own or his neighbour's fence, nor took "a mug o' ale, sociable-like," in the "White Hart" kitchen; a woman who had no answer to give when a neighbour "passed the time o' day," but who scuttled away from her kind as dumb and as wild as a frightened rabbit — who should say which was the least human of these?

So Maher at length crept away, leaving the mother, very old now, crippled with rheumatism and with a chronic asthma, quite alone. To all questions addressed to her she vouchsafed the briefest answer, or, when it pleased her, none at all. She did not know where he was gone, she did not know what he was doing, she did not know if he was ever coming back. As to whether she was sorry to be without him, whether she was afraid to live in such a solitary place alone, whether he had gone away in consequence of any unpleasantness, if he had left her enough money to live on, if he had treated her with kindness while with her — on these points when questioned she was absolutely silent.

It was impossible to get on with the woman, so "onmannerly" was she; and the people, who through curiosity or kindness had valiantly made friendly advances, drew back and left her alone once more.

For years she lived so; alone with her memories of the past, with whatever secrets her life held. By the look of her face uncommonly ugly some of her reminiscences must have been.

As time went on her rheumatism grew worse, so that, by-and-by, she was quite disabled, and lay on her bed groaning and sometimes shrieking with pain. And in the daytime the little daughter of her nearest neighbour waited on her, "riddin' up" her house, cooking her little food, rubbing her poor limbs with the horse-oils upon which the Dulditch people pin their faith for the "rheumatics." But when these duties were fulfilled (with that zeal and discretion to be expected of eleven years) the little maid would scamper off home. She was the eldest of nine, and her parents were among the poorest in the parish — glad enough of the "shillin' a week and her wittles," for which Dora, night and morning, walked the long distance between the "Lost Housen" and her home. But for forty times that sum they would not force the child to sleep in the evil-looking place, falling quickly to decay and ruin through bad building and neglect, where the ghost of the murdered toll-gate keeper still stalked uneasily amid the river fog and the mists.

So that long before the shades of night fell upon the "Lost Housen" Jemima Crouch was left alone.

For a year Dora walked to and from the cottages. Through evenings and mornings, making three hundred and sixty-five days, she trod the "joyless fields" of winter, or waded through the same fields "waist-deep in meadow sweet" in the lovelier half of the year. She made her short cut through the woods from "faather's" to "Mis' Crouch's" when the bright leaves of the chestnut, the fierce, copper-hued leaves of the beech, the lemon-yellow leaves of the elm and the maple were falling softly about her ears with a sound as of pattering rain. She came through the woodland path in the early spring when those glorious-toned leaves lay a moist, smelling, rotting mass beneath her feet, and when the buds on the boughs overhead were aching to open:

> "Ere a leaf was on a bush,
> In the time before the thrush
> Had thought about her nest."

Through the rigours and delights of the year, then, little

Dora ran the half-mile homeward, or walked to the scene of her day's labours with lagging feet. For she had a childish, exaggerated dread of the woman upon whom she waited, lying helpless on the bed, regarding the little maid with her wide, staring eyes, or shrieking horribly upon the stillness in her unbearable pain. There had been days in the early part of her service when the child, going her unwilling errand, had heard those shrieks in the distance and had cowered away in the wood, or hidden among the osiers for hours before she had found courage to go on. There had been foggy afternoons in winter when the mists floating up from the river in the form of a murdered toll-keeper's ghost had pursued the child to the very door of home. Awful experiences of unknown terrors, incommunicable sufferings burdening Dora's mind went to the earning of that shilling which was of so much value to the family comfort.

At last there came a day in winter when Dora, trembling, crying, distraught with fear, appeared in her home circle an hour before her appointed time. She had only an unintelligible tale to tell, and no one could satisfactorily determine why she was so frightened.

There had been a noise in the uninhabited one of the "Lost Housen" of someone moving about there. In the broad light of day, and at first, the child had not been frightened, had even, it seems, offered to Mrs Crouch to discover who or what had taken up abode there, but had been forbidden to stir from the bedside. It was apparently the undisguised terror of Mrs Crouch herself which had communicated itself to her small attendant, increasing in the imaginiative but ignorant mind of the latter to a perfect frenzy of fear of that hidden something moving about on the other side of the thin wall.

Something was there that breathed like the bull "i' Rober'son's midder," Dora said; that stumbled about the floor and fell against the wall like "granfaather when 'e were in drink of a Sat'd'y night"; that was yet more awful a thousand times than the infuriated, bellowing bull or the intoxicated grandparent.

All through the long day the child had supported her terror of the hidden thing, cowering away from the dividing wall that at any moment might open to disclose a sight too awful for little girls to see and live. But when, as time went on, the pale woman on the bed, who had forgotten her pain in her fear, or who had managed to repress all the usual cries, intimated to Dora in a strained and agonised whisper that she dared not be left, that the child must promise for the love of God not to leave her as usual, but to stay at her side all night, for that she was afraid, horribly afraid; when she had clutched at the little hand and arm and had insisted, almost voiceless, but horribly, fearfully impressive, in the hoarse, painful whisper of extremest fear, that not for a moment must she be left alone with what was behind the wall; then the child with a wild cry had pulled herself from the woman's clutches, and, without waiting to look for hat or jacket, had flown from the house and torn homeward as if all the fiends of the bottomless pit had been behind her.

Dora was put to bed, her teeth chattering as with ague, and she screamed all night through at intervals, and muttered in her dreams; and in the morning, to her thankful relief, was found to be too feverish and headachy to start on her usual day's work.

It was Dora's mother, therefore, who on pushing open the door of the ill-fated house discovered the horrid sequel of the unknown terror of the day before.

Upon the bed, scratching and tearing at the air with distorted skeleton fingers, lay Mis' Crouch, the silence she had kept for so many years broken hideously at last by ceaseless babble of maniacal raving. Opposite her bed, hanging from a nail in the wall, was a thing terrible to look upon: the hidden horror of yesterday made visible for the destruction of the senses.

Dora's mother with one wild glance assured herself that what Mrs Crouch was addressing in hoarse confidential whisper, or in loud frenzied entreaty, was not, as she had at first thought, the last year's scarecrow out of the patch of wheat behind her own back door, cruelly maltreated, and hung up to frighten the sick woman. That it was indeed and in truth the dead body of Maher Crouch, who had hanged himself there before his mother's eyes. Then, having with desperate effort summoned strength of mind to slam the door upon the ugly sight, she ran as far as the "White Hart" (where brandy was at hand to recover her) and fainted on the doorstep.

The villagers, who came in a crowd to cut the suicide down, noticed that the rotten wall had given way in several places under the weight of Maher before he had at length found means of firmly fixing the nail upon which to strangle himself. Unpleasant to imagine the sight which must have taken place before the helpless mother's eyes! It was said in Dulditch, where people do not at all shrink from attributing crime or awarding judgment, that the woman's sin must indeed have been great, seeing that her punishment was so terrible.

It is not quite certain if it was from the desire to justify the Power which had so heavily smitten J'mima Crouch, or if it was from the revelations of her own disjointed but incessant ravings that the theory which now maintains about the family was formed. The basis in either case is unsound, for the self-accusations of a maniac cannot be accepted as evidence, and upon perfectly innocent people very heavy misfortunes daily fall.

However the truth may be, it is now held in Dulditch as a fact, undoubted and unalterable as the fact that the world was created in seven days and that Jonah existed for a period in the belly of a whale, that Jemima Crouch assisted her son Og in the attempt to slay his father, and afterwards urged on Maher to murder his brother, and was punished by having to witness the protracted death struggles of the latter, hanging himself with some difficulty before her eyes.

She is very old now, and passes her days in a ward of the pauper lunatic asylum, lying always helpless on her back. But from the way in which her eyes (full of the horror for which perhaps they had kept themselves vacant of expression so long) fix themselves on the white bare wall, and her twisted fingers scratch the air, it is evident she still sees the starting eyes, the protruded, horrid tongue, the blue, hideous face of the son always hanging himself before her.

The "Lost Housen" are lost indeed now. It is little more than a heap of rubbish which marks the place where they stood.

LEVENSES

THE first day of harvest. The sun hot upon the field where the reaper is noisily cutting its broad pathway through the corn. The shadow of the hedge and the two great elms by the gate is thrown black upon the stubble. Within the shade a group of women are seated in the tidy white aprons and with the generally cleaned-up appearance exacted by rural custom at the time of year and the hour when the noontide meal is due. Beside them, in the long dry grass of the bank, where the lavender-coloured scabious, the small scarlet poppy, the slender, wiry mouse-ear sway on their long stalks, the baskets are standing which contain the "levenses" for the workers in the field.

"'Tain't on'y a heavy time for th' men. 'Tis th' wives as bear th' brunt of it," one of the women was saying. "I ha' left my gal, Ireen, to drag th' coach wi' th' little uns and the heaviest o' th' things. She ain't on'y twalve, come Janivary, but she ha' got th' strength o' t'ree o' me."

"You're lucky as you ha'n't only one man to perwide for, tro' th' harvest, Mrs Drake," the woman who sat beside her remarked.

"I ain't none so sure," Mrs Drake made answer. "If so be as you've got t'ree of 'em, Mis' Browne, you ha' th' wages o' t'ree to dale with, remember. And a matter o' fourteen poun', I reckon, a-comin' in at th' ind o' th' harvest."

"Wait, bor, till yours is growed up like mine — for the two boys is as hungry as th'man — and see what they kin ate! — Here come yer Ireen, Mis' Drake, wi' Ronald and th' lessest little boy i' th' cart. Min' th' gate-pos', Ireen," she screamed, as the child in question appeared upon the scene.

"What a keerless little mawther you be!" her mother scolded the new-comer. "You as near as nothin' tarned th' coach over by the pos'. What for d'ye imitate runnin' when th' two little uns is behind ye?"

Ireen, white-haired, red and round and shining of face, was seen to be excited. "Bobby Wapple, he ha' fell down i' th' midder, a-bringin' his father's wittles," she was shouting as she approached, tugging at the long handle of the green-painted go-cart, in which lay two children asleep beneath a bottle, a drinking mug, and a basket of provisions. "He's a-hollerin' like a good un, and th' drink's spilt inter 'is basket."

"Well, I never!" the women said in a chorus, and stared, pleasantly stirred, upon Ireen. Some children seated by their mothers scampered to their feet and flew off to the scene of disaster.

"Kin I go back and pick up th' pieces, and help Bobby Wapple?" the little girl asked.

"No, and can't!" the mother promptly announced. "You stop along o' me, and kape a-jogglin' th' cart wi' the little uns."

"Theer! the cutter's stopped!" another voice cried. "Here come th' men. They'll be riddy for a drink, I'll lay my life on't."

The labourers came, slouching heavily over the golden stubble. They picked up their discarded coats and neck-handkerchiefs from the bank, donning them, or making of them pillows for their heads as they lay down, sprawling beside their wives. One, a neglected-looking man of forty, with a dark and miserable face, a dirty wisp that had once been a necktie, and once been scarlet, binding his torn shirt about his gaunt throat, stood for a minute looking over the group.

"Wheer's my Bobby?" he asked.

"He've fell and broke th' bottle into's basket," Ireen,

anxious to deliver the intelligence, panted out.

"Oh!" He spoke with the soured, dejected air of one habituated to, but not resigned to, the buffets of Fortune, and removing himself from the rest, sat down upon the warm grass amid the gently stirring flowers of the bank. There, his face turned in the direction in which Bobby should come, he waited; while the slices of harvest cake, the slices of bread and cheese, the mugs of drink were dealt out to the luckier men.

"Sarve 'm right," Mrs Drake, with her mouth full, was remarking to Mrs Browne. "Set a little uno' nine yare old to order his wittles, and to kerry 'em! Why don't the man git a woman to do for 'm, and live dacent-like?"

"Tom ha' had enough o' women," one of the men said. "Th' one he'd got runned 'm inter debt, and left 'm to help hisself, poor beggar."

"A matter of eight months ago come the fif' o' September 'tis since Charlotte bust up with 'm and took herself off. A fine time him and Bobby ha' had iver since! And him that proud and shut up he ha'n't niver asked no neighbour to do 'm a hand's tarn."

One of the younger men got up and carried a mug of beer to him who sat alone. He accepted, and drank it in silence, still looking towards the gate through which Bobby should come.

The child appeared at length, but not alone.

"My word!" said Mrs Drake, staring with all her eyes.

"If that ain't Charlotte, I'm a dead woman!" said Mrs Browne. "You may bet your life the hussy have come back!"

The woman to whose skirts Bobby Wapple was clinging passed without any recognition the group of old neighbours and acquaintances on the bank. So set were her eyes and thoughts on the lonely figure beyond, it is possible she did not even see them. She stood before him for a minute, and watched his dark, lean face turn yellow beneath the tan. His mouth dropped open, his eyes stared. But he said nothing, and without a word she slipped to the place beside him on the bank. Bobby, with an anxious look at his father, settled down upon the skirt of her dress.

"Wheer's my wittles?" the father demanded of the boy, who began to whimper.

"I bruk th' bottle, daddy. They're sp'ilt."

"Is they all sp'ilt?"

"Oh, Tom!" the woman said pitifully. "I looked i' th' basket. There weren't nothin' but dry bread theer."

"'Tis on dry bread him and me ha' lived for a matter of eight months—thanks to you," the man said. He turned and looked at her with fierce reproach. "You runned me up bills I thought was paid, to a matter o' fi' pound. Fi' pound! You ruined me; and then you tarned your back, and cut and run; and left him and me to fend for oursel's. And we ha' nigh starved, le' me tell you. A fine mother and wife you be! What are ye a-doin' of here? Who axed ye to come? I swore I'd let my tongue rot out afore I axed ye; and I wull. What are ye a-doin' of?"

"I thought as you and Bobby 'ud be muddled i' th' harvest time. I felt as if I'd got to come and lend a helping hand!" she said, and trembled where she sat.

"I never axed ye?"

"No." He had a grudging and surly manner, but so miserable a look that she could not but be gentle with him.

"Fi' pound!" he repeated. "A matter of fi' pound."

"Theer was the doctor's bill when I was ill i' th' winter; and th' bill that hadn't never been paid when our little Gladys was born. That got me behind-hand, Tom, and I cou'n't never catch up agin. And then theer was you on yer club for two months wi' your sprained back, and not so much, by four shillin's a week, comin' in; and you that hard, Tom, I was afeared to tell ye. So, mother say, 'Lave 'm, and come home'; and I took my Gladys and went. I thought as how you'd come after me, Tom -"

"You might ha'knowed me better," Tom said. "I swore as th' tongue should rot i' my mouth." He paused, raised the mug to his lips, loudly gulped down the beer.

She looked at him, sideways, as he drank: at his thin, hungry face; his ragged clothes. She lifted the neglected and weeping little boy into her lap, and began to cry.

"Tom," she said, "I went because I was afraid. But I haven't been happy without you and Bobby. I don't believe as you and him ha' been happy without me."

He put down the empty mug upon his knee; he looked out at the still uncut expanse of corn: the gold of it grew dim, grew black, was blotted out; the coarse hand he dragged across his wet lip shook.

There was a stir among the group farther down the bank. Ireen had started to bump her go-cart across the meadow to her home; the rest of the children made off to play in the dust of the road, to climb the gate, to hang over the sides of the ditch where the water ran in a tiny stream beneath the tall cresses; the women still sat to talk over their empty baskets; the men slouched off heavily again to their work.

"Tom!" the woman said, and touched Tom Wapple's ragged sleeve.

"The fi' pound is paid off. Me and Bobby well-nigh starved to do it," he said. "You kin stop and bring my fourses i' th' arternune, if ye like."

Morrow & Co, Bungay, Suffolk
01986 893148